IT JUST FEELS RIGHT

HOPE FORD

It Just Feels Right © 2023 by Hope Ford

Editor: Kasi Alexander

Proofreader: Nicole Graf

Cover Design: Lori Jackson

Image Photographer: CJC Photography

Cover Models: Eric + Jackie

CHAPTER 1
CASSIE

"You're joking, right?"

Chloe shrugs and then brushes her long blond hair off her face. She's giving me that knowing look of hers, and I can't help but laugh. "Forget it. No way."

She smacks her hand on top of the wood tabletop in front of me as if she's trying to get my attention. Which is crazy, because since she's dropped her little bombshell, all I've done is stare at her and wonder what the heck she's thinking.

She giggles. "Quit looking at me like that. It's not a completely foreign idea. I mean, it's not like I made up the whole concept. It's a well-known fact, if you want to get over one man, you need to get under another."

I gasp and look around the bar, hoping that no one is listening to Chloe and her asinine idea. She leans back on her stool and crosses her arms over her chest as she gives me a knowing gaze. "No one can hear me. We're in a bar, Cassie. Chill out."

I lean in and loudly whisper to her, "First of all, I'm a brand-new teacher in town. That's all I need is for the Whiskey Run gossip grapevine to tell my principal—who hates me anyway—that I'm hooking up at the Whiskey Whistler." I hold my hand up when Chloe starts to talk. "And don't even try to convince me no one will know. I'm all too familiar with the way things spread here. And second of all, I'm over Richard. I was over him before he cheated on me."

She doesn't believe me. That much is obvious by the way she's looking at me with pity on her face. I lean in. "I'm serious. I should have broken up with him a while back. Catching him with another woman just pushed me along."

She tilts her head and searches my eyes before grabbing my hand and squeezing it. "Cassie, you don't have to be strong with me. You can talk to me. I'm not judging you."

I look around the bar. There aren't many people that know the real me. Brook, my sister, probably knows me better than anyone. And then there's Haven. She has been my best friend for so long she knows any time I'm trying to hide something, and she's always quick to call me on my shit. And then there's Chloe. We were close in high school but sort of lost touch since I went away to college. I've changed a lot in the last four years. I'm not the same woman I was when I left here.

I was insecure and never fit in anywhere. It could have been because my dad was the town drunk and left our family when I was twelve. He stayed in town causing a ruckus for the next three years before he finally left the area and hasn't shown his face since. But the people of Whiskey Run haven't forgotten it. It didn't help that my mom was known as "the woman that changes husbands like she changes purses."

So yeah, when I started college, I left Whiskey Run and swore to myself I would never come back. But here I am, four years later, living with my mom and her new husband, teaching at the local elementary school. I didn't realize when I left that I would miss this small town and would find my way back here.

I blow out a breath. "Okay, Chloe, listen to me."

She's shaking her head. "It's fine, Cass. Really. We don't have to talk about it, I just want you to know I'm here when you're ready to get it off your chest."

I grab her hand to stop her from going on. "Listen, I promise, I've been over Richard for a while now." I roll my eyes. "He'd been pressuring me to have sex with him since our second date, and I knew... I knew I didn't want to lose my virginity to him—"

She cuts me off and exclaims loudly. "Your virginity!"

I lean over and smack my hand over her mouth. "Really? Really! Do you think you can say it a little louder because I don't think the people heard you over at the pool tables."

She's shaking her head side to side. "But... but you're what, twenty-two? How are you still... I mean, there's nothing wrong with waiting... I guess I just assumed."

I shrug. "Look, I'm not trying to be weird about it. I have trouble connecting with people—you know that about me—and well, I'm not doing THAT with someone unless I'm completely comfortable with them so yeah, I was not going to have sex with him." I lift my shoulders up. "And that's why he cheated on me. Or so he says. I know the truth, though: He's an ass."

Chloe is staring at me with her mouth hanging open. "Wow."

I bark out a laugh. "Geez, it's not like I'm some old maid or something. I'm twenty-two and I just haven't found someone I want to do that with yet. It's not a big deal."

She nods in agreement. "You're right. It's not. I'm sorry I assumed."

I shake her off. "Don't. You don't owe me an apology for anything. Now can we please change the subject?"

She waves down a waitress and asks me, "What do you want?"

After the last few days I've had, I'd love to have a drink to take the edge off, but again, I don't want my principal to hear I've been drinking in town. "I'll just have a soda."

Chloe scrunches her nose up, and when the waitress comes over, she points at me. "Cassie will have a soda, and I'll take a Long Island iced tea."

The waitress just nods her head. "I'll be right back."

When she disappears, I nod my head toward a man at a corner of the bar. "Let's talk about how you keep staring at that man over there, surrounded by all his buddies, and he hasn't taken his eyes off you since we sat down."

I have to give Chloe credit. She doesn't even look his way, but her cheeks do turn a pretty red. "I don't know what you mean."

I barely resist rolling my eyes. "Oh really? You don't know what I mean? That's funny, because you've been looking at him all night too."

She shakes her head, and it's obvious she's doing her best to not look that way. "I have not."

"Whatever, Chloe. Look, it's okay. You can talk to me. I'm here if you need someone to—"

She cuts me off. "Forget it. I think he works for Walker or something. He's definitely military, and knowing how those guys are, he won't be in town long…"

When her voice trails off, I scoot to the end of my seat. "But you like him. Admit it."

She doesn't deny it. "It doesn't matter. All he does is stare at me. He never comes over and talks to me."

I look over at the man, and he is in fact staring at Chloe again. "Uhhhh, you're wrong. That dude is so hot for you, he can't stand it."

The waitress brings our drinks back and sets them down in front of us. After we tell her thanks and she walks away, I take a big sip of my soda as Chloe twirls the straw in her drink. "Trust me, he's not. We're just friends."

"Bull—"

I'm cut off when two men stop next to our table. "Hey, ladies."

They say it plural, but both men have their eyes on Chloe. I don't begrudge it, though. Chloe is beautiful inside and out. She's like a Barbie doll with her petite figure, long blond hair and big blue eyes. I take a drink of my soda and watch everything unfold in front of me.

Both of the men are vying for Chloe's attention, and it's obvious she's not comfortable, so I cut in. "Hey boys, uh—"

I start to interrupt them, but in a split second, they've turned on each other. The first one slurs, "I told you, I got the blonde."

I bite onto my lip and tug my fingers through my red hair as the other man replies in a matching slurred voice, "And I told you redheads don't do it for me."

Chloe is staring at me wide-eyed. She hates confrontation, and so do I, but I've had to deal with it my whole life, so there's no way I'm going to just sit here and take it. I stand up from my chair. "Hey, you two, can you take yourselves somewhere else?"

But neither one of them is listening. They've moved to where they're standing almost against each other, talking in low tones, but I know it's going to escalate quickly. When one pokes the other in the chest, I move to stand between them. It's definitely not my smartest move, but here I am, all five foot four of me, pushing my way between the two of them.

I try to nudge the two apart, and I'm not sure exactly what happens first, but I hear Chloe scream my name, I feel myself being pushed, and I put my arms up, but I'm not quick enough.

The pain in my head is intense, but I don't lose consciousness. At least I don't think I do. I hear yelling, what sounds like a table being knocked over, and then I'm sitting in a chair with Chloe hovering over me, and the man that is always watching Chloe is now hovering over her.

I put my hand to my head and wince, but at least there's no blood. "I'm okay."

Chloe gasps. "You're okay? You just tried to break up a bar fight. I think you're far from okay."

There's a grunt from the man, and he's staring at Chloe like he's about to throw her over his shoulder and carry her out of here. Yeah, he's definitely into her. I push Chloe's hands off me. "I'm fine. I could go for some ice or something maybe. I really don't want to have to explain a bruise on my forehead at school tomorrow."

Chloe gives me a look. "Uh yeah, sure. I can get some ice."

"Stay. I'll get it," the man says. He takes two steps and turns back toward Chloe. "Don't move." He gestures to his buddies, and if I read the look right, he's telling them to watch her.

There's still a little chaos around us. The two guys that started the fight have been dragged out the door, so now I'm just dealing with everyone looking at me. Yep, my boss is definitely going to hear about this.

When the man comes back, he hands the bag of ice to Chloe. She tries to hold it to my head, but I take it from her and push it gently on my bruise. "What happened anyway?"

The man gruffly explains, "The one asshole pushed the other asshole, and he grabbed on to you and took you down with him."

"Uh, the police are here," Chloe says.

Darn it. Of course the cops would come. I mean, why not? Can this night get any worse?

I follow her gaze, and sure enough, there's a man in blue coming my way. I do a double-take as I look at the man walking straight toward me. His eyes are glued to me, and I'm sure he's just here to check on things, but I'm feeling all kinds of personal about it. He's tall and handsome. I know I shouldn't, but I let my gaze travel down his body. He's muscular, and he looks good in his uniform. When my eyes go back to his face, he's openly smirking at me. It's almost as if he knows exactly what I'm thinking.

My whole body gets at least ten degrees hotter when he stops in front of me, and all I can do is stare up at him, hoping I don't make an even bigger fool of myself.

CHAPTER 2
BAKER

SHE IS the most beautiful woman I've ever seen.

As soon as I walked into the building, I saw her, and I couldn't look away. I know she's the one I'm looking for, it's a given with the ice she's holding to her head, but it wouldn't matter anyway because I'm not letting her out of my sight.

As I get closer, I see Chloe and Elias, one of Walker's mercenaries, standing next to my girl. And yes, I haven't even talked to her, I don't know her name, heck, I don't know anything about her, but I know she's mine. Or she will be, anyway.

I stop next to Elias and position myself right in front of the injured woman. She's looking up at me with her mouth hanging open. She's affected by me, that much is obvious.

I lean down because I need to be closer to her. Bent over, I search her face. Without saying a word, I reach for the bag of ice in her hand and lift it from her head. She blinks up at me, speechless. I wince when I see the knot that's already formed on her forehead. "Oh baby," I grunt.

Her eyes widen, and I realize I called her *baby* out loud. She looks down, and that's not going to do. I like having her eyes on me. I put my hand at her chin and raise it gently until her eyes meet mine again. "Talk to me. Are you okay?"

I try to make sure I'm holding her gently even though anger is pumping through my veins. "Can you tell me if you're okay?'

She nods, but I shake my head. "Words. I need to hear you say it."

Chloe leans in. "Cassie, what's up, girl? Tell him you're okay. Oh God, is she in shock or something?"

Cassie… her name is Cassie. Something clicks, and I deflate for just a second. Surely not… this can't be THE Cassie.

She shakes her head and looks at her friend. "No, I'm not in shock. I'm fine."

Her hair falls across her face, and I clench my hands at my sides to stop from reaching for her and brushing it away. I want to be able to look at her face.

She smiles softly and finally looks at me again. "I'm okay. It was my fault."

Elias grunts next to me, and it's obvious he disagrees with her. I would be jealous, but everyone in town knows that Elias likes Chloe. "It wasn't her fault."

I don't have to look at the other man. I already knew it wasn't Cassie's fault. Anyone could look at her and know it would never be her fault. She's too sweet and too innocent looking. "Do you want to press charges?"

Her gasp tells me her answer before she mutters a word. She starts to ramble. "No. Definitely not. It was my—"

I growl at her, and it surprises us both. But I'm even more surprised when she reaches for me, touching my hand as if she wants to reassure me. "No, really. I mean, those men were not nice, and they were starting to fight. I hate fighting, and I thought I could stop them, but I know, I know. I should have minded my own business. But they were fighting over Chloe, and she was uncomfortable—"

This time it's not me that interrupts her, it's Elias that puts his hands on Chloe's shoulders and pulls her to him. "You should have come and got me."

They start talking, but I tune them out and do what I've been wanting to do since I got here. I put both hands on Cassie's shoulders. "What can I do for you?"

She doesn't tense up. If anything, she leans into me. "I'm okay."

I pull up a stool and sit down, putting her legs between mine. "Do you think you can get up?"

She nods her head, and then as if she remembered my request from earlier, she says, "Yeah, I really am fine."

"Your pupils look okay. Any pain or nausea? Did you lose consciousness?"

She smiles and shakes her head. "I promise I'm okay. I'm more embarrassed than anything."

I'm about to shake her off and tell her that she shouldn't be embarrassed, but she giggles. "And what? Besides being a cop are you a doctor too?"

I scoot closer. I love that she feels she can joke with me. "No, I'm not a doctor, but I would love to get you checked out by one. Just to make sure you're okay."

She firmly shakes her head side to side. "No, I don't need a doctor. It's a bruise and no big deal."

I'm about to insist when she starts to shake her head. "Look, I'd really just like to go home."

Chloe reappears and sits down next to Cassie. She's watching me, no doubt trying to figure out why I'm sitting so close to her friend. She puts an arm around Cassie. "I'll take you home."

Cassie is quick to decline. "No, you stay and have some fun. I can call my sister to come get me. She won't mind."

"No." I practically yell at her and then shake my head at myself. *Real smooth, Baker.* "I mean, it's fine. I can take you home. I'd like to talk to you a little more about the incident anyway."

She gathers her hair at the nape of her neck and then wraps it around her hand, baring her neck to me. Already I can imagine pressing my lips to her soft skin. She releases her hair with a soft huff. "There was no incident. The one pushed the other and I guess he grabbed me when he started to fall."

Chloe's head is rolling back and forth between us, and she must figure it out on her own. She nods her head. "Right. You should let the uh, the officer, take you home."

I blink at her because she knows me, she knows my name... and she knows who I am in relationship to Cassie. Somehow I'm going to have to break it to Cassie, but I want to let this play out as long as I can.

"You going to let me take you home?"

She gestures to me. "You're working. You don't need to take me home. I can get a ride."

She tries to get up, but with me crowding her, she can't. I put my hands on her knees. I'm not only breaking every rule right now but I'm doing it and not giving a fuck. Which should scare the hell out of me. I'm a by the books person, and I always follow the rules. But I guess if it comes to touching Cassie, I'm going to break each and every one of them. "I would like to take you home."

She's watching me with curiosity, and I smile at her. She has to be able to see how badly I want to spend time with her. "Go with me. I won't sleep tonight unless I know you've made it home, safe and sound."

"But..." she starts just as Chloe starts to talk.

"I know you haven't been back home long, but I can vouch for him. Ba—uh, the officer is a good guy. You know I wouldn't let someone take you home unless I knew you'd be safe."

When she still hesitates, Elias jumps in. "And I'll make sure Chloe gets home, so don't worry about her."

Finally, I let out a breath as Cassie nods her head. "Okay, sure. Thank you. I really am ready to get out of here. Plus I have school tomorrow."

That's when I try to recall everything I've ever heard about Cassie. She's a teacher over at the middle school. She is twenty-two years old, ten years my junior. She doesn't have the best relationship with her mom, at least to hear her mom say it. She's really close with Brook, her sister. But even knowing all that, it's not enough. I want to know everything about her. I stand up. "Do you want me to carry you out?"

She bolts to her feet. "Carry me? No way. I'm already going to be the talk of the town, I definitely don't need people saying that a cop had to carry me out of the bar."

I frown, and even though I don't like it, I offer, "If you're embarrassed to be seen with me, I can wait for you outside."

She jerks back. "Embarrassed? No, that's not what I meant. I mean that I don't want people thinking I'm drunk—or in trouble—and you had to carry me out."

I nod. "So I can walk next to you?"

She laughs and smiles as if she's surprised by my request. "Yes, you can walk next to me."

I want to ask her if I can hold her hand, but I hold back. I would love for everyone in this bar to know she's mine. That way the whole town will know it by tomorrow. But I need to bide my time and not scare her off. She literally just met me and has no idea who I am. I can't help wondering when she figures it out, will it blow every chance I could have had with her?

And even though I don't hold her hand, I do stand protectively next to her while she hugs Chloe bye. I nod my head at her and Elias, and then because I can't resist, I put an arm around Cassie's waist to help her to the door.

She doesn't resist me, and I breathe a little easier as we walk out of the bar into the cool night air.

CHAPTER 3
CASSIE

AFTER HE HELPS me into the front seat of his squad car, I watch as the police officer walks around to the driver's side. As soon as he shuts the door, I'm thanking him again. "I really appreciate you driving me home."

He hasn't started the car yet. He has his left arm over the steering wheel and he's turned facing me. "I wasn't joking earlier. I won't sleep tonight unless I know you've made it home safe."

Maybe I'm being too naïve. "You don't think those guys will bother me, do you? I mean, I was just trying to get them to stop fighting, that was all."

He grips the steering wheel. "Those two won't come near you, Cassie. If they do, tell me, and I'll take care of it."

When he says my name, it's like a little thrill goes through me. I cross my arms over my chest because my breasts feel full and achy all of a sudden. My mouth is suddenly dry, but I force the words out anyway. "Okay, thank you."

After he stares at me for another moment, I start to fidget in my seat. The chemistry between us is like nothing I've ever felt before. "Uh, will you get in trouble taking me home when you're supposed to be working?"

He just shakes his head. "No. And I wouldn't care if I did."

I nod, accepting what he's saying. I want to ask him if he feels this too, but I'm not brave enough. I'm sure every single woman in Whiskey Run hits on him, and I don't want to just be another woman throwing themselves at him.

He pulls out onto the street, and I hate knowing that it won't take very long at all to get home.

"Are you okay?"

We're at a stop sign, and he's looking at me questioningly. "You were sighing. Are you okay?"

I nod. "Yeah, I'm fine."

"Are you glad you're back in Whiskey Run?"

I almost ask him how he knows I left and came back, but I figure he's probably just heard it from someone tonight. "Yeah, I am."

He taps his hand on the steering wheel. "You sound surprised."

"I guess I am. I thought when I left to go to college, I would stay gone, but I missed it here. I missed my sister."

He nods his head in agreement. "I can see that. Your sister is a good person."

This time there's no hiding my surprise. "You know my sister?"

He nods but changes the subject. "You like teaching at the middle school?"

And all at once, I remember. I think my face was numb from the ice, but since he's brought it up, I pull the visor down and open the mirror. It's dark in the car and I can't really tell so I push the visor back up. "Yeah, I love it actually, but I probably won't have the job after tomorrow."

He tenses and straightens up in his seat. "What do you mean you won't have a job tomorrow?"

Even though I know he can't really see it in the dark car, I still point to my forehead. "This."

His arms flex as he holds on to the steering wheel tighter. "What? You'll lose your job because you got hurt?"

My voice is shaky because I'm filled with worry. I really don't want to screw this up. "Yeah, when my boss finds out I was in a bar fight, she'll fire me. She hates me."

He reaches over and pats my leg, and I sit perfectly still, wishing he would keep his hand on me. Geez, what the heck is wrong with me? I'm never like this. He grunts and pulls his hand away. "It's going to be okay. And you weren't in a bar fight."

I laugh because just the image of me in a bar fight is kind of funny. I'm laughing now, but I know I won't be tomorrow. "Trust me, by the time Mrs. Daniels hears about it, she'll have heard I was drunk, I hooked up with some random guy, and then got into a bar fight. She's just looking for a reason to fire me."

"Mrs. Daniels? Are you kidding? Krista Daniels is still the principal at the middle school?"

I nod. "Yeah, how did you know that? Wait, what do you mean still? I thought you were new to Whiskey Run."

I turn in my seat, completely focused on him now. He's watching the road, and it gives me time to take him all in. He's slow to respond, but I don't mind. "No, I'm not new to Whiskey Run. I lived here most of my life. I've been gone for a while working undercover in Jasper, and I just got back last week."

I hold my hands together in my lap. *Don't ask. Don't ask,* I repeat to myself but it doesn't stop me. "How old are you?"

He smirks and looks over at me. "Thirty-two." He pauses. "Ten years older than you."

"How do you—"

"How do I know how old you are? I know a lot about you. I didn't know when I met you that I'd want to know more, though."

My lower belly pulls as he hints that he wants to know me better. I can barely process it before he says, "Is that a problem?"

"No, I'd like to know more about you too."

His smile is instant as he looks over at me. "And the fact that I'm ten years older than you? Is that a problem?"

I bite my lip to stop from begging him to take me now. I don't know what's come over me, but sitting here with… Oh my God. "Uh, no it's not a problem. I'm sorry. You seem to know everything about me, but I know nothing about you. What's your name?"

For the first time since I've met him, he frowns. It's then that I look out the window and realize we're sitting in the driveway at my mom and stepdad's house. "Uh, how did you know where I lived? How do you know so much about me?"

He turns in his seat, and I can't figure out why he's looking at me the way he is. He almost looks disappointed. He opens his mouth but doesn't get a word out because there's a knock on the car window. I lean forward and see my stepdad standing by the car. I'm sure he's probably worried that there's a cop car in his driveway.

"Fuck," the man sitting next to me says before rolling down the window.

My stepdad leans down. "Hey, son. I'm glad you came by."

"Son?" I practically shout. I point at the stranger, the man that I'm most definitely attracted to, and ask him in shock, "You're Baker Johnson? You're, uh, you're my stepbrother?"

He winces. "I'm Baker Johnson."

I open my mouth, close it, and then open it again. "Uh, okay, well, thank you for the ride." I get out of the car and am walking around the front of it when my stepdad looks at me. "What happened? Who did that to you?"

I appreciate his concern, I really do. I've only been home a month, and I was surprised to discover how much I liked my stepfather. He's a really good guy. But I definitely don't want to get into everything that happened. Especially after the little bomb that just sort of exploded in my face. "No one did it to me. I did it to myself."

Ryan puts his hands on my shoulders. "Honey, you got a knot on your head. Who do I need to kill? Baker, were you there when this happened?"

Baker is out of the car and comes to stand beside me. He pulls me gently until I'm out of his dad's arms and turns me so we're facing each other. I do everything I can to try and avoid looking at him, but he's too hard to resist.

He ignores his dad and instead talks to me. "It's already bruising, Cass. Make sure you take a pain reliever before you go to bed tonight."

I nod, but a part of me wants to cry. I've never had anyone be concerned for me, not like this, and of course, the one man I'm attracted to ends up being my stepbrother. I pull back, and with my back straight, I start to walk away. "I will. And thanks again. Good night, Baker. Good night, Ryan."

I turn on my heel and practically run up the walkway and inside the house. My mom is sitting on the couch watching television, and I don't even bother stopping to talk to her. I know she'll give me some kind of speech about how tonight was my fault, and I don't want to hear it.

I jog upstairs and go to my bedroom, shutting the door behind me before I toss myself onto the bed. With a groan of frustration, I roll to my back and stare up at the ceiling.

It's just my luck. I finally have a connection with a man, and he ends up being my stepbrother. He's off limits... no matter how much I wish he wasn't.

CHAPTER 4
BAKER

MY DAD HAS his arms crossed over his chest, just watching me. I've never been able to hide things from him, and I'm not going to try to now. "What? Go ahead. Ask me."

He gestures to the house. "She okay? Do you know who did that to her?"

"There was a fight at the Whistler. She was trying to break it up, and one guy pushed another and the guy took Cassie down with him when he fell. That's how she got the bruise on the forehead."

He chuckles, and I shake my head. "What's funny about that, Dad?"

"Your sister. I swear she's a spitfire. There's not many women that would interfere with two grown men fighting."

He's right about that. She is a spitfire, and I've never met a woman like her. But I still hate that he's referring to her as my sister. I don't have any brotherly thoughts about her at all.

"You want to come in?"

I don't... but I do.

I've only been back in town for a week, but I've avoided coming to see my dad and his new wife. The truth is, I don't really care much for Brandi. I've tried to be nice to her, but it's hard. I'd only been around her a few times before I went to Jasper for the undercover job, but those few times were enough to let me know that I want to limit my time with her. I was fortunate enough to miss the whole wedding performance since I was working undercover. But no matter how much I don't want to see my stepmother, I don't want to miss a chance to see Cassie.

"Sure. I'm still on my shift, but I can come in for a minute."

My dad doesn't try to hide his surprise. I follow behind him, and I'm holding my breath the whole way. In mere seconds, I'll see Cassie again, and hopefully I can explain things to her.

I practically shove my dad to the side when I get in, hoping to see Cassie, but the only one sitting in the living room is Brandi.

She does a double-take when she sees me, and for just a brief moment I see the displeasure on her face. I know she doesn't like that my dad and I are close, but she's quick to hide it. "Baker… what a nice surprise. You doing okay?"

"Yeah… where's Cassie?"

She turns back to the television. "Oh, she went out tonight."

I roll my eyes as Dad starts to tell her about what happened. I wait for Brandi to express her concern or to get up and go check on her, but she does nothing except shrug her shoulders. "That girl. She's always looking for trouble."

I grit my teeth. Yep, I like her even less now.

"Hey, Dad, I'm going to use the restroom. I'll be back."

My dad gives me a knowing look. "Sure thing, son."

I bypass the bathroom on the first floor and take the stairs two at a time. I walk down the hallway to the bedroom that I know Dad and Brandi had talked about giving Cassie when she came back from school. The door is shut, and I want to push it open, but I knock softly instead.

There's a rustle behind the door, and then it swings open. Cassie gasps and rears backward. "Baker? What are you doing?"

I walk into her room and shut the door behind me. She's already changed clothes, and I let my eyes trail down her body. The shorts and tank top do nothing to hide her from me. I fist my hands at my sides because I want to reach out, grab her by the hips, and pull her flush against me. "I had to make sure you were okay."

She nods, eyes wide, looking between me at the closed door. She looks trapped, and I hold my hands up. "Hey, I'm sorry. I can leave."

She crosses her arms over her chest. "Why didn't you tell me that you… that we're…" She blows out a big breath. "Why didn't you tell me that you're my stepbrother? I thought…"

I take a step toward her, wanting her to continue. "You thought what?"

She uncrosses her arms and slaps her hands on her thighs. "Forget it. It doesn't matter now."

I move before I can talk myself out of it. My hands go straight to her hips, and I pull her against me. She fits me perfectly, but I knew she would. "You thought that I was attracted to you… that I'm interested in you."

She juts her chin at me. "I did, but I didn't know that my big brother was just playing me."

I lean down until our lips are only inches apart from each other. I keep one hand at her waist, and the other comes up and wraps around her neck. Her pulse is racing under my thumb, and I rub it back and forth. "I wasn't playing you. I want you."

She swipes her tongue across her lower lip, and I groan. She has no clue that I'm barely hanging on. She sucks in a breath, and I feel her pebbled nipples cut across my chest. Fuck me.

She tries to pull away, but I don't let her. "Baker, you're my step—"

I cut her off. "Don't say it. We're not related."

My little spitfire rolls her eyes. "We are… you're my—"

"I'm yours. That's how you should word that sentence… Tell me you're mine."

Her hands go to my chest, but she doesn't push me away. "Baker, we can't… we shouldn't."

"Baker! You okay, son?" my dad hollers up the stairs.

Cassie tenses, and I reluctantly let her go. "Yeah, I wanted to check on Cassie. I'll be right there."

She pulls from my arms and hisses at me, "Baker… They're going to know you're in my room… they're going to wonder what we're doing in here."

I put my hand on the door to stop her from opening it. I lean down, pressing my lips softly to the bruise on her forehead before pulling away. "We're just talking… tonight. Even though I'd give anything to stay in here with you the whole night, I can see you need some time to warm up to the idea."

She can try to deny it all she wants, but I see the way her eyes light up. She may not want to feel what she's feeling, but it doesn't change the fact that she wants me. And that right there is all I need right now. "I'll see you tomorrow."

I open the door, and without another look back, I walk out of her bedroom. The only reason I don't look at her is because it's nearly impossible to walk away now. If she gave me any indication she wanted me too, I'd stay. Fuck everyone else because from this point forward, whatever Cassie wants, Cassie gets.

As I come down the steps, my dad is waiting at the bottom. The look he's giving me is knowing, and I'm sure he's wondering what I was doing, but I don't care. I wait until I'm standing next to him. "Make sure she takes some Tylenol for her head. Call if she needs anything." I put my hand on his shoulder and squeeze him affectionately. "Love you, Dad. Talk to you soon."

I get to the door before he stops me. "Son."

I knew he wouldn't let me off the hook so easily. That's just not who he is. "Yeah, Dad?"

He comes closer, and I notice that Brandi is still sitting on the couch with her full attention focused on the television. My dad's voice is hushed. "Is there anything you want to tell me?"

I shrug. "What do you want to know?"

I wait, holding my breath. It's obvious that I'm interested in Cassie. He'd have to be blind to not notice it, and of course, I'm worried he's going to try and forbid it or tell me all the reasons why it's a bad idea. But he surprises me. "Don't hurt her."

I shake my head. Did I just hear him right? "Did you just tell me not to hurt her?"

He lifts his head and looks me in the eye. "That's exactly what I said. Cassie is special."

I nod. Even though I just met her, I already know that. "I know she is, Dad."

He shifts his feet and positions himself between me and the door, stopping me from leaving. He crosses his arms over his chest. "I'm serious. I see that look in your eye. I'm telling you, she's special. Don't start something that you don't plan on finishing. Do you understand what I'm telling you?"

I don't even blink. I search his eyes, and I don't know what to say to him to convince him, so I say the first thing that comes to mind. "She reminds me a little bit of Mom."

He looks shocked for just a second, and so I continue. "She took on two men bigger than her because she didn't want them fighting. She cares about others more than herself. She was worried about her friend having to leave to take her home. She cares about her job, her sister. And I just met her tonight, Dad. Trust me, I know she's special."

He must realize that I'm being sincere because he moves to the side. "Okay. Have a good night, son, and don't be a stranger."

I walk out into the night. "See you soon, Dad."

Because sure enough, I'll be spending some more time here.

CHAPTER 5
CASSIE

I FEEL LIKE HELL, and I know I look it too.

I tossed and turned most of the night, replaying in my mind the moment Baker walked into the Whiskey Whistler until he walked out of my bedroom. One thing I discovered was that the attraction I felt wasn't just one-sided. He was definitely more vocal about it and didn't act as if he was going to back down. But who knows, in the light of day, he could completely change his mind. Plus, I have so many questions. One being, did he know who I was the whole time?

But I can't worry about it now.

No, now I need to worry about getting into my class and avoiding Mrs. Daniels. With my head down, I walk briskly into the building. I have to walk right past the office, and I normally wave and say hello to the school secretary, but today I'm looking straight ahead, hoping to avoid everyone.

I get two steps past the door to the office and my shoulders start to release from their tensed position when I hear my name being bellowed. "Miss Waters. Can I see you please?"

I tremble as panic hits me. I want to run in the opposite direction, but I know I'm just putting off the inevitable. I hold my papers and folders closer to my chest, shake my head so my hair falls over my forehead, paste a smile to my face, and then walk into the office. "Hi, Mrs. Turner." I nod at the secretary, and she gives me a sympathetic look. Shoot, they know. I knew they would find out, but who would have thought they would know at seven o'clock the very next morning? I walk into Mrs. Daniels' office. "You wanted to see me?"

Her eyes go straight to my forehead. I know she can't see it. Not only is my hair covering it but I piled on the makeup this morning. The swelling is completely gone, and the bruise is hidden underneath layers of concealer. Mrs. Daniels isn't fooled, though. She comes around her desk and stops in front of me. "Do you have something you need to tell me about last night?"

I open my mouth but don't get a word out because she immediately starts talking again. "Miss Waters, do I need to remind you that we have a code of conduct here? We don't just ignore it when we hear about our teachers running around in bars, drinking and getting into brawls."

I remind myself that I want to keep this job. There are three schools in this town, elementary, middle, and high, and if I get fired from one, I won't be able to work at any. And I really don't want to go to Jasper to work at a school there. "Mrs. Daniels, I'm well aware of the code of conduct, and that's why yes, I met a friend last night, but I did not drink, and I definitely did not get into a brawl."

She crosses her arms over her chest. "I heard otherwise."

I let out a breath and start to explain. "There were two men that started to fight. I was just trying to stop them, and that's it."

She's staring at me as if she can literally see right through me. I don't know if she's waiting on me to change my story or what so I pace my breathing and keep looking right back at her.

She tilts her chin up at me. "You do know that we will find out the truth."

I nod even though I don't know if that's true or not. One thing about Whiskey Run is that the gossip mill sometimes runs amuck, and she may only hear embellished truths. "I understand. Can I get to class now? I need to get some planning done."

She purses her lips together. "Fine. But I promise you that I will be looking deeper into this, and if I find out that—"

I move my folders to one arm and hold my free hand up. "I understand."

She gives me a firm nod and waves her hand as if she's dismissing me.

I turn on my heel and walk out. I make it to my class without any further incident, but the little talk with Mrs. Daniels lies heavily on my shoulders all day.

I go through the motions, and there are only a few instances throughout the day where it's obvious other teachers must have heard about the previous night. They of course got a good laugh about it, but for me, it's impossible to find the humor in it all.

It's now the end of the day, and my friend that teaches next door steps into my classroom. "You okay?"

Charlotte has been a great friend to me and has really shown me the ropes around here. I sigh and shrug my shoulders. "Well, I still have a job, if that means anything. I mean, if I'm fired, they haven't told me yet."

"You're not going to be fired."

She barely gets the statement out when the intercom in my room buzzes. "Miss Waters?"

I hold my breath. "Yes."

"Mrs. Daniels would like to see you please."

I fall into my chair and rest my head on my desk. Dammit. "Okay," I mutter.

"Excuse me?" the secretary says.

I lift my head off the desk, and in my most pleasant voice, I tell her, "Okay, I'll be right there."

I slowly stand up, and Charlotte meets me in the middle of my classroom and hugs me tightly. "It's going to be okay. I promise. Even if you get a reprimand."

She holds her hands up when I open my mouth. "And I know you didn't do anything to get reprimanded; I'm just saying that they're not going to fire you. There's no one to fill your spot right now."

I roll my eyes. "Well, that makes me feel better. They're not going to fire me because they're waiting for someone to fill my position. Thanks for that."

Charlotte laughs and shakes her head. "You're worried for nothing. It's going to be okay. Do you want me to go with you?"

I shake my head. "No. There's no sense for Mrs. Daniels to tie you to me in any way. She still likes you."

Charlotte pulls her bag up her shoulder. "Are you sure? I parked out back, but I can take the long way around and walk with you."

I shake my head. "No, it's okay. I'll see you in the morning."

She pats me on the back, and we go in separate directions. I make the long trek down the hallway toward the offices. When I get to the front office, I stop suddenly when I hear Mrs. Daniels laughing from her office. What the…? I don't think I've ever heard her laugh. I go to the open door and am about to knock when I spot Baker standing inside, smiling and looking as charming as ever. He's in uniform again, and he looks even more handsome than I remember.

It's then that Mrs. Daniels spots me. The whole walk here I prepared myself for a tirade, and I was ready to defend my actions from last night. But I don't get a chance to.

Mrs. Daniels comes toward me with her arms wide open. I tense up because I'm not sure what's about to happen, and she wraps her arms around me as she laughs and hugs me. "Cassie," she admonishes as she pulls back and looks at me. "Why didn't you tell me that you are friends with Baker? He told me he was there last night and you were completely innocent."

I meet Baker's eyes, and he's looking at me with a satisfied smile on his face. I'm completely stunned by the turn of events. Baker walks over to me and puts his hand around my waist, effectively pulling me away from Mrs. Daniels. "Mrs. Daniels—I mean Krista—it was so good to see you again."

She blushes. Stone cold Mrs. Daniels is blushing. "Oh my, you too. And how sweet are you to come in today to talk about the carnival. All the kids love your dunking booth."

I look at him in shock. "You do a dunking booth for the school carnival?"

He looks almost sheepish. "Yeah, I think it's good for the police to be seen around the school and to have a good rapport with the kids. I had to skip it last year because I was undercover, but I'm looking forward to picking it up again."

My heart starts to race in my chest. Can this man be any more perfect?

Baker nudges me toward the door. "Well, we're going to head out of here. I know you've had a busy day, so we'll let you get to it. Thanks again for meeting with me, Krista."

I wave over my shoulder. "Good night, Mrs. Daniels."

She calls back in a giggly tone, "Night, Baker. Have a good night, Miss Waters. I'll see you in the morning."

I almost trip over my own feet on my way out of the office. We get down the hall before I can form a sentence. "What just happened back there? What did you do to her?"

CHAPTER 6
BAKER

I LAUGH and point in the different directions of the four-way hallway. "Which way to your classroom?"

She points to the left, and I walk by her side, my hand on her hip. "I didn't do anything to her, by the way. Mrs. Daniels has always liked me."

"And you decided today is the day you wanted to come and talk to her about the dunking booth?"

My hand tightens. "No, I came today to clear up any misunderstandings about last night."

"You mean she called you?"

I shake my head. "No, I called her."

She stops outside a classroom. "Is that the only misunderstanding you wanted to clear up?"

I peer down at her, and my heart constricts in my chest. I thought about her all night, trying to figure out this obsessive attraction I have for her. Even now, I can't explain it, but I know I can't just let her go. "You mean last night… with me and you?"

She nods, holding her breath. She looks worried and tense, and that's not how I want her to feel when she's with me. I want her to feel safe above all else.

"This you?" I ask, pointing at her door.

She nods, and I put my hand on her lower back. "Yeah, let's talk about last night's misunderstandings."

We walk into my classroom, and she stops abruptly. "Colby! What are you doing in here?"

He jumps out of his seat and stands facing us. His face goes white when he sees me standing next to Cassie. "Miss Waters! I thought you left already."

Cassie pulls away from me and walks toward him. "What are you doing here, Colby?"

He shrugs. "My mom was late picking me up, so I thought I'd sleep a little until she got here." He pulls his phone from his pocket. "I'm sorry. I know I shouldn't be in here. I'll go… my mom… She should be here soon. I'll go wait by the front doors."

Cassie stops him from leaving. I'm watching them closely, trying to figure out the situation. I know Colby. For the most part, he's a good kid. But there are issues at home. Cassie is speaking to him softly. "Colby, it's okay. I'm fine if you're in here, you just have to let me know. You can wait here."

The kid looks at me again and shakes his head. "No, that's okay. I'm going to go. I'll see you in the morning."

Something is not right. I know Colby's been having trouble at home, but there's obviously more to it. Cassie must realize it too. "I'm going to leave soon, and if you're still here, I'll run you home, okay?"

He nods his head. "Okay, bye, Miss Waters. Bye, Officer Johnson."

"See you, Colby," I call after him.

Cassie looks worried, and I ask her, "You're worried about him, aren't you?"

She nods immediately. "Yeah, I understand it's just him and his mom, but there's more to it. I just don't know what I can do to help him."

I can't tell her everything I know about the mom. If Cassie is worried now, she'd be even more worried then. I try to reassure her. "I'll check on him when I leave here before I go to the station."

"Okay, thank you." She moves to the other side of her classroom and leans against her desk. I hate that she's putting distance between us, and that's obviously what she's trying to do. She tilts her head to the side. "Can I ask you something?"

I tell myself I should stay where I'm at, but I can't help it. I walk over to her, stopping just a couple of feet away. "You can ask me anything."

She nods, crossing her arms over her chest. "When did you realize I was your stepsister? Is this some kind of game? You want to mess with your dad or my mom or something?"

My jaw tightens. "You think I'm messing with you?"

She shrugs, but her eyes remain on me. "I don't know what to think."

I take a step toward her and then another. When I'm standing right in front of her, I reach for her arms and gently unwrap them from across her chest. I let my hand trail down her arms and then thread our fingers together so I'm holding her hands between us. "I knew the first moment you saw me. Do you remember it?"

She laughs with a little snort and then stops suddenly, embarrassed. "Yes, I remember. I wasn't drinking, and it was just last night."

"Did your heart start to race?"

She rolls her eyes. "I just got body-slammed to the floor. My heart was racing."

I smile knowingly. "Did you feel a tremble start at your neck and then it rolled through your whole body?"

Her eyes widen, but she shrugs. "I was holding ice to my head. Of course I was trembling."

I'm not stopping. "Did your nipples pebble? Was there a tug in your lower belly that you didn't quite know how to deal with? When you were sitting in front of me, your knees between mine, were you thinking about having my hands on you?"

She gasps, and her voice trembles when she asks me, "How did you? I mean—"

She doesn't finish her sentence, so I lean down and am so close it's a fight within myself to not just kiss her. "How did I know what you were feeling? Because I was feeling it too. Every bit of it and probably more graphic than you imagined."

I pause and take a deep breath. "Cass, when I first saw you, I didn't know who you were. I just knew that I wanted to know more. When Chloe called you Cassie, I put two and two together and knew that you were my dad's new wife's daughter."

She laughs at my wording. "Your stepsister... I'm your stepsister."

I shake my head. "You can put whatever name you want on it. All I want to hear is, you're mine."

She pulls a hand from mine and slaps me gently on the chest. "Stop. You have to stop this. Nothing can come of me and you. We can be friends, and we'll see each other at family events and around town, but that's all we can be."

I cover her hand with my own, pressing it to my heart. I know she can feel my heart racing. "Can you look me in the eyes and tell me that you don't feel anything for me?"

"Baker, I just met you last night."

I bring up my other hand and wrap it around the base of her neck. "I know we just met. I'm asking you if you feel anything for me."

She's speechless as she blinks up at me. My voice softens, and I lean in, pressing my forehead against hers. "Tell me you don't feel anything for me and I'll walk away, Cass."

I can see her mind whirling. I'm sure she's thinking about her mom, my dad, her sister, family gatherings… everything. That's who she is. She wants to take care of everyone. "Baker."

I groan, and my hands tighten. "Say it again."

"Baker… we can't. I want to, but I can't."

"Can I kiss you?"

"No…" she says and then quickly changes her mind. "Yes."

I want to devour her. "Cass, baby, I need you to give me an answer. Can I kiss you?"

She clenches her eyes together, and I forget to breathe. When she opens them, I can see the answer in her big green eyes. "Yes."

I don't hesitate. My lips are on hers in an instant. First just small kisses and then I run my tongue along her seam with a moan. "Open for me, Cass. Let me in.'

When she opens her mouth, I take full advantage. I tilt her head to the side, deepening the kiss. My whole body reacts to having her in my arms, flush against my body and her lips captured by mine. The kiss is everything.

There's a slam of a door from somewhere down the hallway that jerks us apart. She pulls out of my arms and is panting, trying to catch her breath. She's looking at me, and I see the shock on her face. I'm just as affected by it, and I reach down to adjust my hard manhood. Her eyes watch my every move, and when she licks her lips, I feel it as if she's touching me instead.

She moves away from me, her eyes panicked. "I need to go, Baker. I have to go."

I go after her, but she holds both her hands up, palms out, to stop me. "Don't you dare. If you come over here, we're going to kiss again, and we can't."

I mimic her and walk toward her slowly. "We are going to kiss again, Cass. There's no way after I've tasted you that I won't do it again."

I see her tremble from my words. "Baker—"

I groan and start patting my chest, right over my heart. "Fuck, I don't know what it is, but when you say it, it hits me right here, baby."

She whimpers. Fuckin' whimpers, and for just a second, I think she's going to give in, but she shakes her head, backing away from me. "I'm leaving, Baker. This is crazy, and it's all happening too fast. I need to go."

I physically deflate, but I force a smile to my face. I'm not giving up, but I can give her time. "Okay. I'll walk you out."

She picks up her bag and purse, and before she can sling it over her shoulder, I tuck it over mine. "I'm ready when you are."

She snickers. "Uh, I don't know if it matches, Baker."

I put a hand at the small of her back. "Har, har. Funny."

We walk through the school. There are a few teachers we pass, and they say hello, and it's obvious they're curious about me walking with Cassie.

When we get outside, Cassie is looking up and down the parking lot. "Colby's not here."

I try to reassure her. "Maybe his mom picked him up. I'll go check on him before my shift."

When we get next to her car, she holds her hand out for her stuff. When she grabs it, I don't let it go. "I want to kiss you again, Cass."

She wants to. That much is obvious, but she's still fighting it. "I can't, Baker. I need to think about this and figure it out."

"I'm not giving up, Cass. You need to know that."

Instead of answering me, she tugs on her bag. I release it and open her door for her. She tosses the bag over to the passenger's seat and then sits down. She looks at me, and I realize I could get lost in the green with gold flecks of her eyes. "Thank you for helping me with Mrs. Daniels. And well, everything."

I lean over. "I'll see you soon, baby."

I shut the door and watch as she drives away. The whole time, I'm trying to figure out when I'm going to see her again and what I'm going to do to win her over.

CHAPTER 7
CASSIE

I NEED to forget about my stepbrother.

I've told myself that very thing for the past two days, but here I am, daydreaming yet again. He's coming to dinner tonight.

My stepdad dropped that little bombshell on me last night, and I've been anticipating it ever since.

"What can I do to help, Mom?"

She gives me that look, and I grit my teeth. "I mean Brandi." I don't know what her thing is, but she has it in her head that she looks more like my sister than my mom and that it will confuse people if I call her Mom. The truth is, it confuses people when I call her Brandi. Everyone knows she's my mom.

She swats her hand at me. "You know I don't like help in the kitchen. Why don't you set the table."

I grab a stack of plates, and she reminds me, "Set an extra place setting."

I try not to blush. "Okay, yeah, Ryan said that Baker is coming."

She rolls her eyes. "Yeah, well, I've invited a guest too. So set another one."

I don't like the way she said it. I know when my mom is up to something, and she definitely is right now. "Who's coming to dinner?"

She shrugs. "You're so nosy."

I'm not worried about upsetting her now. "Mom, what have you done?"

I wouldn't put it past her to have invited my ex. She was extremely upset that I broke up with him, and let's face it, inviting him to dinner would be something that she would do.

The doorbell rings, and I move in front of my mom. "Who did you invite to dinner?"

She's not intimidated, though. She walks past me. "Well, let's just go see."

I follow behind her, trembling mad. I don't have a clue who it is, but I'm guessing I'm not going to like it. She knows I won't cause a scene. I always just bite my tongue and go with the flow.

When she opens the door, I go into the dining room and start putting plates out, fuming mad. I hear their voices and the surprise in my stepdad's voice. Obviously, he didn't have anything to do with this. I listen intently, and I hear my mom call him Roger. I start wracking my brain trying figure it out, and it hits me. My gynecologist. She invited my gynecologist to dinner. Oh my God!

They all come into the dining room as I finish setting out the plates. Roger comes over to me, and I can't even look him in the eye. Mom stops next to me, pinching me on the fat of my arm. "Cassie, you know Roger O'Dell. I thought it would be nice for you two to meet since you're so close in age and local professionals."

I'm shocked at how my mother would think this is a good idea. "Mom, uh, I know Dr. O'Dell. I'd say he knows me really well. He's my gynecologist." I sigh and can't keep it in. "He's seen my hoo-haa."

Ryan barks out a laugh but stops when Brandi silences him with a look. Roger pulls at the collar on his shirt, and my mom pinches my arm again. Fuck me, how is this happening? I hold my hand out. "It's nice to see you again, Dr. O'Dell."

He laughs and shakes my hand. "You too. You can call me Roger."

I pull out of his hold, and without glancing at anyone, I say, "I'll be right back. I need to grab another place setting."

Ryan stops me. "This is fine, Cassie. Baker called and said there was some kind of emergency, and he wasn't sure if he'd make it."

I nod and try not to let my disappointment show. "Okay, well, I'll go and help Mom bring food in."

I walk into the kitchen, and when my mom comes in, I turn on her. "Mom, what are you thinking? I do not want to be fixed up with my gynecologist."

She hisses back at me, "You ungrateful little..." Before she finishes, she pulls herself together and puts a smile on her face. It's almost scary how she can be a crazy woman one second and then switch to smiling "mom of the year" next. Not that her words match, though. "Look, you can't live here forever."

I shake my head. "Mom, I've been here for the summer. I'm saving up to get my own place. I should be able to get something by my next payday."

"You wouldn't have to work if you married a doctor."

I'm shocked. "Mother, you honestly don't think I'd want to date someone because they're a doctor, do you?'

She points at the serving dishes on the counter. "Not date… marry."

"Mom, this is ridiculous. I'm not going in there."

She gets that look in her eyes. "You will too. You live in my house, so you live by my rules."

She grabs a plate of chicken. "Now pull yourself together, daughter. The men are waiting for us."

And just like that, she puts a smile on her face and walks out of the kitchen. I wish my sister didn't live in a two-bedroom apartment with three other women. She's offered for me to stay anyway, but I thought by living at home I would be able to save money quicker. I didn't realize it would be hell, though.

Ticked off, I grab the bowl of mashed potatoes as Ryan walks into the kitchen. "You can do better."

I laugh. I'm not sure how my mom convinced Ryan to go out with her because he is amazing. "Thank you. Too bad my mom doesn't think so." I point toward the other room. "Did you know Mom was setting me up on a blind date today?"

He shakes his head and sighs. "No, I didn't."

I lift my shoulder. "You know I don't plan on sponging off you forever. I almost have enough money saved to get a place."

"Honey, you can stay here as long as you want. Take your time. If you move out now, you'd have to pay rent, and that would just be a waste of money. Wait, save up some money, and then you can buy the house you want."

My mouth drops. "You mean that, don't you?"

"Of course I do. Now we'd better get out there. Come on, I'll help run interference."

He grabs the bowl of green beans and plate of rolls, and I follow him to the dining room. My mom laughs when we walk in. "I thought you all got lost or something."

Ryan goes to set the food on the table. "Just making sure we got everything. Everything looks great, Brandi."

She takes the mashed potatoes from me. "Quit standing there like a lump on a log, sit down." I take the seat across from Roger and wait for my mom to tell me to move or something.

Plates get passed around the table, and I keep reminding myself that it's one meal. After we eat, I'll have a talk with my mom about the whole blind date thing.

We eat and talk, and I want to hug Ryan as he keeps Roger talking so I don't feel any pressure.

Roger is in the middle of talking about some new golf clubs he got when the doorbell rings. Ryan turns to me. "I bet that's Baker. I tell him to use his key, but he won't anymore. Do you mind getting it?"

I'm out of my seat in an instant. I don't know why, but I'm a nervous wreck the whole way to the front door. I take a deep breath and open it.

He looks tired, but his face lights up when he sees me. "Hey, baby."

I gasp and look behind me. "Baker, you can't call me that."

I move back so he can come in. "They're in the dining room. Go sit down and I'll grab you a plate."

I move toward the kitchen and am surprised that Baker followed me instead of going to the dining room. I'm not going to argue with him, it will be pointless. "Your dad said there was an emergency. Are you okay?"

He leans against the counter and brushes my hair off my shoulder. "Were you worried about me?"

I shrug. "I'm glad you were able to come to dinner." It's then I remember. "Oh yeah, I should probably tell you something."

"What's that?"

I grab a plate and busy myself getting a cloth napkin and some silverware. When I have it all, I walk toward the door. "Uh, my mom fixed me up on a blind date. He's… uh, here now."

He's not happy. His jaw tightens, and his lips flatten. "Did you want to be fixed up on a blind date?"

I scrunch my nose up. "Uh, no. Of course not."

He nods and comes to stand next to me. "That's right. Because you're mine." He leans down and kisses me briefly on the lips. "Come on. Let's go meet this date."

Shocked by that kiss, I just follow behind him. "Look who showed up."

I catch my mom's eye, and she's obviously not happy. Baker isn't fazed, though. He waits until I sit down and then sits down next to me. I start passing him bowls so he can plate his food. The table is quiet, and I realize that Baker is giving Roger a dirty look. "Uh, Baker, this is Roger. Roger, this is Baker."

Brandi interjects, "Yes, Baker is Cassie's brother."

I can't help it. My nose scrunches up, and I insist, "STEPbrother."

Baker reaches under the table and squeezes my knee. I jerk in shock, and he nods at me approvingly before smirking at Roger. "So, Roger, do you live in Whiskey Run?"

He nods. "I do. I'm a gynecologist over at the new medical offices at the edge of town."

My mom starts to laugh. "He's Cassie's gynecologist."

I don't even have to look at Baker, I know he's not happy with this news. I look at my stepdad, pleading with my eyes to help out, but he's just smiling ear to ear, looking between Roger and his son.

"Soooo…" I start, hoping to change the subject.

Baker points at the man across the table with his knife. "He's your… doctor."

I nod. "Yep."

His knuckles are white as he holds the knife, and I'm starting to fear for Roger's life right now. "Yeah, so what happened at work, Baker?" I ask him, trying to change the subject.

He searches my eyes, and I plead with him silently. He sets his knife down, reaches under the table, and puts his hand on my leg again. He's holding on to me and doesn't let go while he talks. "There was a wreck out on the highway to Jasper."

I suck in a gasp. "Is everyone okay?"

He squeezes my leg. "There were injuries, but they're going to be okay."

"Good, that's good."

He reassures me, "I just had to help direct traffic. They'll be fine, though."

I nod, and everyone starts talking. I breathe a sigh of relief since the topic of Roger being my gynecologist is no longer being discussed. However, I stay on high alert. I have no idea what my mom will say at any given moment, so I need to be mentally ready.

"Cassie."

I realize that Roger is trying to get my attention. "Oh, I'm sorry. Yeah, Roger?"

He clears his throat and looks around the table before settling his gaze back on me. "I was thinking after dinner we could go catch a movie."

I open my mouth to respond, but Baker beats me to it. "She can't."

I jerk my eyes from across the table to Baker next to me. "Uh…"

I can feel my mom glaring at me. Everyone is looking at me. The old Cassie would just do what my mom wanted. I don't know what it is or why I'm always wanting her approval, but as I look into Baker's eyes, I know I can't do it. There's no part of me that wants to. "He's right. I'm sorry, Roger. I can't."

CHAPTER 8
BAKER

Brandi leans forward and asks loudly, "What do you mean, she can't? She can do anything she wants, and I'm sure she'd love to go to the movies with Roger."

I stare at her, wondering what's up with her. Anyone that knows Cassie would be able to see that she's been uncomfortable the whole time she's set here.

My dad tries to help. "Now, honey, maybe we should…"

She cuts him off. "She's my daughter, Ryan and I know what's best for her."

I can't help but take offense. I'm a police officer, and Roger is a doctor. I don't begrudge Brandi if she wants Cassie to have a good life, but I don't think that's what this is about. "I'm sorry, Brandi, but Cassie already has a commitment tonight."

She looks at her daughter, and I lean forward to block Cassie from seeing her angry gaze. "She can't because we are serving on the carnival committee, and we have a meeting tonight."

"Carnival committee?" she snarls. "Why would you be helping with the carnival?"

"I do a booth there every year."

My dad chimes in. "His dunking booth makes the most money of any booth there."

I nod and turn to Roger. "Yeah, so we have a lot of planning to do. I'm sure you understand, Roger."

Roger is watching Cassie, and I wish I could block him. I don't even like him looking at her.

Cassie clears her throat, and her voice is a little shaky when she starts to talk. "Yeah, uh, Roger. Actually, I think you're a great guy, but I think it might get awkward if we go on a date since you're my doctor."

I glare at the other man and dare him to pressure her. All it takes is for him to say one thing that's inappropriate and I'll climb over this table to get to him.

He opens his mouth, looks at me, and then nods his head. "Yeah, sure. I completely understand, Cassie."

I sit with one hand on Cassie's knee as Brandi excuses herself. It's obvious she's mad. Cassie stands up, brushing my hand from her leg. "I'm going to go help Mom bring in dessert."

As Dad starts talking to Roger, I get up and follow Cassie and her mother into the kitchen. I don't trust my stepmom, and I'm not really sure what kind of relationship they have, but I do know I'm not going to stand by and let Cassie get upset.

As soon as I get into the kitchen, I see Brandi cornering Cassie against the counter, and when she hears me come in she steps away and turns to me. Her smile is instant, but it's too late. I've already seen the pure evil on her face. I position myself next to Cassie. "Cass, I'm sorry to do this to you, but I'm going to need to get to it. Do you think we can skip dessert so we can get to our meeting?"

She's overwhelmed, that much is obvious, and she has been since I got here tonight. I hate it and that's one of the reasons I want to get her out of here. She nods and sighs in relief. "Of course, I'm sure you're tired after working a full shift too. I'll grab my purse."

I wait for her to go and without a word to Brandi, I walk back into the dining room. "Dad, Cassie and I are going to go ahead and go. We have work to do." I look at Roger and hate that my parents brought me up with impeccable manners. "Roger."

My dad stands up. "Roger, I'll be right back." He follows me to the front door, where I wait for Cassie. I'm on high alert because if Brandi goes looking for her, I'll be following.

My dad is looking around the empty entryway. "Everything okay? What's going on?"

I grit my teeth. I have done my best not to talk shit about his wife, but man, it's hard. "Nothing, Dad."

He spits out, "Bullshit. Talk to me. Is Cassie okay?"

I nod slowly. "Yes, she's all right. I'm not sure what the hell your wife was thinking trying to fix her daughter up with that man."

He holds his hands up. "I'll talk to her and tell her no more blind dates."

I want to punch something, but I know it's not my dad's fault. The poor guy is innocent in all this. "Okay, sure, thanks, Dad."

Cassie comes down the stairs. "I'm ready. I should probably go—"

I cut her off. "It's okay, I've already told them bye for us."

My dad nods his head. "It's fine, honey. You two have a good night. Let me know if you need a ride or anything."

I roll my eyes. He has been the best dad ever, but seeing him as a girl dad has been something else. I like that he's protective and caring over Cassie, though. She needs all the people on her side she can get. I put my hand at the small of her back and help her out the door. My dad waves bye to us, and Cassie starts to walk to her car. "I'll follow you since I'm not sure where we're going."

I laugh. "Nope, you can ride with me."

She jerks to a halt. "Baker, that's ridiculous. You know you're tired, and you're not going to want to drive all the way over here to bring me home. I can just drive."

"Cassie," I say sternly.

She reaches out and wraps her hand on my forearm. "I'm just thinking about you. You look like you're dead on your feet."

I cup her cheek. "Will you please ride with me? I want to spend as much time as possible with you."

She takes a step back and looks up at the house. "I'll ride with you. But this isn't a date. I appreciate you getting me out of that sticky situation, but this is us working on the carnival together."

I let out a breath and walk around to the passenger side of my squad car and open the door. "You're the boss."

She comes to get in and stops next to me. "You mean that, don't you?"

I shrug. "Of course I mean it. I haven't hidden the fact that I like you, Cass, but ultimately whatever happens between us is up to you."

She seems more than satisfied by my answer as she gets in my car. I only live two neighborhoods away, and as I pull into the driveway, she leans forward to look out the window. "Is this where you live?"

I nod. "Yeah. Why? You seem surprised."

She doesn't wait for me to come around to open her door; she gets out and meets me at the front of the car. "I'll withhold judgment until I see the inside. I mean, you are a bachelor. Am I going to see bean bags in place of a couch?"

I laugh and lead her up the stairs to my front porch. "I think you'll be pleasantly surprised."

I open the front door and wave my arm for her to go in. She steps in and looks around in awe. "Baker, this is gorgeous."

I try to see it through her eyes. I've always liked the open concept. The kitchen is like a chef's dream. There's a large couch in the living room in front of the fireplace and a big screen television in the corner. Everything is tucked away and clean looking. "Baker! This is amazing. Did you decorate all this or did you have help?"

I put my hands in my front pockets. It's been five years since my mom passed, but I still think about her every day. "This is one of the last projects my mom and I did together before she passed."

The smile on her face drops, and she comes to me, wrapping her arms around her middle. "I'm so sorry."

I thread my hand through her hair and hold her head against my chest. "Thank you, Cass."

She pulls back, and I reluctantly let her go. She goes to sit on the couch. "Tell me about her. The few things your dad has said about her makes me think she was pretty amazing."

I blow out a breath. "Yeah, she was. Uh, do you care if I shower my workday off first?"

She leans back on the couch. "Absolutely. Go take your time. I promise not to snoop while you're in there."

I start to leave the room and stop. "You can snoop all you want. I have nothing to hide."

I leave her with that and then go to the bedroom. I shower quickly, not because I'm worried about her finding anything but because I want to be able to spend as much time as possible with her.

I walk back into the living room in jeans and a T-shirt. I sit next to her on the couch and face her. "So... my mom."

She shakes her head, frowning. "You don't have to talk about her if you don't want to, Baker, I just thought—"

I reach over and grab her hand. "She was a wonderful mom. She loved me more than anything, and she was always there for me. She was funny, a little nerdy, but man she was fierce." I pause. "You remind me of her a little bit."

She points at herself. "Me? I'm not fierce."

I roll my eyes. "You tried to break up a fight between two grown men."

She groans. "Ugh, I'm never going to hear the end of that, am I?"

I cover our hands with my free one. "I'm just saying… you're pretty badass, Cass."

CHAPTER 9
CASSIE

"You really think I'm fierce?"

He's holding my hand and letting his fingers caress my wrist. "Yes. I do. I also think that you have my dad wrapped around your finger."

I smile as I think about his dad. He has been one of the highlights in my life since I've moved back to Whiskey Run. "I love your dad."

He nods in approval. "He's the best."

I frown as I think about something that has been worrying me. I'm probably betraying my mom by saying this, but I don't hold back. "I don't want him to get hurt."

Baker tilts his head to the side. "How do you mean?"

I avoid his eyes because I feel guilty. If my mom hurts his dad, he's going to blame me somehow. "I don't know what you know about my mom, but this is her fifth marriage." I blow out a breath and don't know how to explain it. "I'm not saying that my mom doesn't love your dad, but…"

He just watches me, no pressure to continue, just lets me form my thoughts. "From my experience, if my mom loves someone, it's not always a good thing. She loves on her own terms."

He clears his throat, and it's obvious he doesn't want to offend me. "I can see that about her." He's tracing my fingers, and goosebumps form on my arms. "What about you, Cass? How does she love you?"

I laugh. "Yeah, well, I think you witnessed that when you walked into the kitchen. She doesn't like it if she doesn't get her way."

He scoots closer to me. "Is that what that was? She was unhappy that you told Roger you didn't want to date him?"

I nod. "Yeah, she wants me to move out. She thinks I'm sponging off her and your dad."

He pushes a piece of hair off my face. "Anyone that knows you knows that's not true."

I look at Baker in awe. It amazes me that he seems to know me better than my own mother. "Does it bother you to talk about your mom?"

He leans in, and I can feel the heat from his body envelop me. "No. What do you want to know?"

"What were your mom and dad like together?"

He reaches up and rubs the scruff on his chin. "They loved each other."

At my blank stare, he continues. "I mean, they argued but never over anything big. They were completely devoted to each other. They were best friends, but they were more. I never questioned if they loved each other. They did. But they loved me too. I've always known that no matter what, they would have my back."

I nod and try not to let the jealousy settle in. I would give anything to have parents like that. Or to just have someone on my side like he's saying. My sister is probably the closest thing I have to that.

"What about you? I mean, I know your mom. What about your dad?"

I laugh. "Well, he's nothing like yours. He was a drunk. He left when I was twelve, but he made sure to stay in town until I was fifteen. I mean, I never saw him or anything, but he kept the townspeople up in arms with all his drunk shenanigans, so that was fun. But yeah, I haven't seen him since he left."

"I'm sorry, Cass. He's the one missing out."

I nod. "Yeah, I know. It's fine. Trust me, I've had a long time to get over it."

There's a brief silence, and I hate it. I'm feeling all the feels as I think about my dad and all that, so I plead with him, "Can we change the subject? Let's talk about something else."

He nods and doesn't even have to think about it. "Let's talk about Roger."

I scrunch my nose up and shake my head. "Do we have to?"

His hand goes to my shoulder. I've never met a man like him before, but he's definitely touchy-feely. It seems that he just wants to have his hands on me at all times. His fingers trail across my collarbone. "He's seen you. I mean, seen you seen you."

I roll my eyes. "He is my doctor."

He nods. "Yeah, and he wants to date you."

I laugh and snort at the same time. I cover my face up, embarrassed, as he laughs with me. "I love that...

I love when you laugh and don't hold anything back."

I roll my eyes. "You mean snort."

He pulls my hand from my face. "I love it. Don't cover your face from me."

I nod in agreement. "Yeah, he's seen my hoo-haa, and he wants to date me. That's weird, right?"

He shrugs. "I don't like it."

I open my mouth, but he interrupts me. "Hear me out. I don't like the idea of any man seeing you." He holds his hand up when I start to talk. "But I know… he's your doctor. But it's different knowing he's attracted to you."

I nod. "I agree."

He searches my face. "So I think that if you want to keep the doctor, I'll go with you to your next appointment."

I bark out a laugh. "You want to go to my gynecologist appointment with me?"

"If you're going to him, yes, I do."

I can't help but laugh, but he doesn't join in. He's serious. I should probably hate that he's so protective of me, but it actually gives me a warm gooey feeling inside. "Well, we have almost a year before my next appointment, so we've got time to figure it out."

He seems satisfied with that answer by the way he leans back against the couch. I scoot back and pull my hand from his. "We should probably talk, Baker."

He tenses. He sits up straighter, pulls his shoulders back, and looks at me with curious eyes. "We can talk about anything."

I nod and try to figure out what I need to say. "So… what are we doing here? What is this?"

He starts to reach for me and then stops himself. "I think you know what this is, Cass."

When I get nervous, I ramble, and it seems today isn't any different. "Honestly, I wish things were different. I wish we could get to know each other and not have to worry about my mom, your dad, my sister, our families. It's just too much, and it adds too much pressure." I jump up from my seat and move across the room to pace. "Maybe we should just talk about the carnival. That's what we came here to do, right? Let's just do that. I need to figure out what my class booth is going to be. I was thinking maybe a fishing booth or something. You know where they put a magnet on the end—"

"Cassie. Stop. Breathe."

I stop pacing and take a deep breath.

He stands up and comes for me. He's walking slowly and deliberately, and I tense up the closer he gets. I already know that I'm weak when it comes to Baker. We are not a good idea. I know we're not, but I don't know if I'm going to be able to resist him. Or if I really want to.

He stops in front of me, toe to toe. I lean my head back to look up at him, and he's searching my face. I'm almost scared of what I see in his eyes. He's bringing out all my emotions, and I'm not sure what to do with them.

CHAPTER 10
BAKER

I CAN'T STAY AWAY from her. I know she's struggling with the fact that she's my stepsister, but I just can't walk away from her.

I want her, and I haven't hidden that fact from her. Heck, my dad knew that first night. But it's more than that. I want to protect her, to spend time with her and get to know her. I want to be able to hold her hand and kiss her anytime I want.

She's peering up at me, and with her unguarded expression, I feel like I'm the king of the world. She doesn't realize it, but her eyes reflect exactly how she's affected by me. She wants me, but it's more than that. She trusts me, and it makes me want to give her everything her heart desires.

"I want to spend time with you, baby. I know you're scared, and a part of it is because I'm your stepbrother, but there's more to it."

"I won't lie to you; I wish we could date but—"

"Good. Then tell me, do you feel like there's something between us?"

She sighs in frustration. "Do you realize you just met me a few days ago? You're willing to jeopardize our whole family dynamic because you what? Because you want me?"

"This between us is more than just me wanting you."

She's clueless. She really has no idea that it's more than just sexual attraction between us. She throws her hand up in frustration. "Do you know how crazy you sound? We. Just. Met. You don't even know me."

I put my hands on my hips. "I know a lot about you. You're a good person."

She rolls her eyes, and I can't help but smile. "Your students love you and know you care about them if Colby is any indication. You've completely won over my dad. All the shit with your mom and your dad, you haven't seen what a good relationship is like or what it's capable of. You don't trust easily, and you don't trust how you feel about me."

She juts her chin at me. "How do you know I'm not exactly like my mom? Maybe I'm trying to win you over."

I search her face, and I can see right through her. There's a part of her that's scared she's going to be like her mother. Maybe that's why she's so scared that this could be something real. "You're nothing like your mom, Cass."

She seems unsure even though I'm absolutely positive about it. I repeat it, hoping she believes me. "You are nothing like your mom."

She shrugs, and even though her body language says she doesn't care, it's obvious she really wants to believe what I'm saying. "You don't know that, Baker. Anyone that knows me knows I'm trying to get out of my mom's house. How do you know I'm not trying to take advantage of you and move in here?"

I laugh and point around my house. "You can move in here."

She rears back in surprise. "Baker! I'm joking. I'm not trying to manipulate you."

She looks so freaked out I do the only thing I can think of. I reach for her and bring her up against my body. Our bodies fit perfectly together. I cup her face in my hands, and I don't ask for permission this time. I lean down and kiss her. She opens her mouth, and I slide my tongue along hers. She whimpers, and I deepen the kiss. It's not enough, though. I let go of her face, slide my hands down her body to her hips, and lift her up. Her hands grab on to my shoulders, and she pulls back from the kiss. "Baker, I'm too heavy."

"You're not. Fuck, you're perfect."

I carry her back across the room and then sit down on the couch with her straddling my lap. She wiggles her hips, and I lift up, pressing my hard cock against her core. She bears down on me and strokes her hips back and forth before she freezes. Her gasp fills the room. "Baker!"

My fingers dig into her hips, and I pull her even closer, lifting my hips. She leans forward, pressing her breasts against my chest. "Kiss me, Baker."

She doesn't have to ask me twice. I press my lips to hers, and my whole body trembles from how intense it is. Kissing Cassie is an addiction. I let my hands slide to her back and hold her to me. She's as close as can be but not close enough.

She pulls away, breathless. Her eyes are round, nose red, and lips swollen. She's looking at me as if I have three heads. "It's never… I mean, you really know how to kiss."

I run my thumb across her swollen lip. "It's not me, Cass. It's us. It's good because it's us."

A worried look comes over her face. "You know that I was joking. I'm not trying manipulate you to like me so I can get away from my mom."

I nod. "I know that. That's not who you are."

She looks at me with doubt, and I know I need to find a way to reassure her. "Cass, baby, you're nothing like your mom. You have a good heart. You're independent, and you would never try to hurt someone else."

Her hands slide from my shoulders up to my neck. "What do you want from me?"

I don't even have to think about it. "Give us a chance."

She shakes her head. "We shouldn't."

I can feel her trying to put a wall up between us, and I'm not going to let her. "Forget the stepbrother thing for just a minute. Do you like me?"

She laughs. "I feel like you should pass me a note and I should check yes or no."

"If you'd rather I do that, I can."

She bites her lip. "Okay, yeah, I like you, you seem like a good guy."

Encouraged, I ask her, "And do you want to get to know me?"

CHAPTER 11
CASSIE

HE HAS SO much hope in his eyes. I know he doesn't see the problem with this, but I've always worried about everything. But I also don't think I can just tell him no and walk away. I'm more than attracted to him, and I want him like nobody's business. I've never been attracted to a man like I am to him. I honestly didn't think I was capable of it. I always thought there was something wrong with me. But right now, with me sitting across his lap, I can feel the pull of desire in my loins.

I try to play it off. "Well, Baker, we are family. We probably should get to know each other."

He shakes his head. "I told you to forget about that. Tell me, Cass. Do you want to know me? The real me?"

I try to push off his lap, but he doesn't want to let me go. I run my hand along his shoulder. "We need to talk about this, but I can't do it on your lap. I can barely think straight."

"Okay, I'll let you up while we talk, but I'm not letting you go far."

I laugh as I climb off his lap, and he pulls me onto the seat next to him. "Okay, talk."

He repeats his question. "Do you want to know me? The real me?"

I fiddle with the hem of my shirt. "Why are you doing this? My mom is married to your dad." I point between the two of us. "Nothing can come of this."

He doesn't realize how hard this is. It's nearly impossible to keep resisting temptation. It would be different if I didn't feel anything, but Baker makes me feel so much. Heck, too much. It's overwhelming.

He grabs on to my hand and holds it like he doesn't want to let me go. I raise my head and look into his eyes. He's searching my face, and it feels like a caress. Almost like he's trying to memorize my features or something. The longer I look into his brown eyes, the harder it is to keep saying no. Impossible really. I look at a frame on the wall above his head, and he knows exactly what I'm doing. "Look at me, Cass."

I bite my lip and shake my head.

He laughs, puts his hands on each side of my face, and pulls me gently down until I'm looking him in the eye. "From the moment I laid eyes on you, I felt something, Cass. I don't know how to explain it. I think about you all the time. All I'm asking is for you to give me a chance. Give us a chance."

Emotion fills me, and I know I can't deny him. Heck, I don't want to. "If we do this, we need to keep it between us."

He doesn't like it, that much is obvious, and he puts voice to his displeasure, shaking his head. "No, I'm not going to act like we're doing something wrong and we need to hide it. I want the whole damn town to know we're together."

I've never known a man to be so vocal. Not ever. He knows what he wants, and he's not afraid to go for it. But even though I appreciate how possessive he is of me, I know what I should do. "Baker, listen to me. When we break up, I don't want it to mess with our family. We need to be able to be together without any more pressure than necessary. We need to just see where this goes."

He shakes his head. "You're already breaking up with me?"

"I'm not. I'm just saying there's a really small chance this is going to work out between us, and there's no sense letting it completely mess up our future family Christmas celebrations or birthdays or anything else. We try this and just see what happens."

He searches my face, and it's obvious he wants to argue with me. He blows out a breath. "If that's the only way I can get you to agree, that's fine. We'll try it your way. But you need to remember that it was your idea to hide this and keep it a secret, Cass. If it was up to me, everyone would know."

I clap my hands on my legs. "Okay, so what does this mean? How we going to do it?"

He scoots back on the couch and lies down. "That much is easy. Any free time we have, we're going to be together. I'm going to date you… well, as much as you'll let me. I guess with your big 'secret dating' idea, we can't go out in town?"

I smile at him. "I don't know. Can you keep your hands off me if we do?"

He shakes his head. "Absolutely fuckin' not."

I laugh and smack him on the leg. "Right. Well then, yeah, we won't be going on dates in town."

"Okay, so you'll come here."

I nod, letting out a breath. "Okay. And maybe we should do a few rules or something."

He nods and points to the space between him and the back of the couch. "Okay. Come up here, and we can talk about it."

I shake my head. "I'm not going to fit—"

He cuts me off. "Woman, are you going to argue with everything I say? You're going to fit perfect, right next to me on this couch. Now come here."

I point at the small space. "You want me there?"

He grabs my hand and tugs me until I'm falling across his body. I giggle as I slide to my side. He positions me as if I weigh nothing at all and my head is cradled on his shoulder. His leg is fitted between mine, and my breasts are pressed against his chest. I stretch my body and snuggle closer to him. "Is this good?"

He puts his hand at my waist and pulls me even closer. "This is perfect."

"Okay, so rules. I think while we're doing this, we should probably not be dating anyone else."

I hold my breath, waiting for him to disagree. He leans down. "Baby, you're crazy if you think I'm even going to look at another woman. It's not happening."

I can't help but think about my whole life. The number of men my mom has had in the house, the times she's cheated on her husbands or they've cheated on her. Hell, Baker's right, I wouldn't know what a healthy relationship looks like if it was right in front of my face. "Okay, but if you decide you want to—"

He cuts me off with a kiss. It's way too short, but he gets his point across. "It's not happening."

I nod. "Okay."

His fingers are underneath the hem of my shirt, stroking the bare skin of my belly. I can barely form a thought, but I want to go ahead and get it all out. "Also, there's something else you should probably know."

We're so close I can't look away. The only thing I can see is him. "This is embarrassing, Baker. Don't freak out."

He tenses, and it worries me a little. Is he going to react how Chloe did the other night? Or is he going to kick me out and tell me he's changed his mind? There are so many things I'm thinking I'm second-guessing if I really need to tell him or not.

"Tell me."

I gulp. "You know what. Maybe now's not the best time to talk about it. Just forget it."

He leans in and rubs his nose against mine. "I'm not forgetting it. You're not getting out of it that easy. Tell me."

"I, uh…" I let my voice trail off. "This is so embarrassing."

His hand comes up, and he cups my cheek. "Tell me."

While looking in his eyes, I do it. Well, I at least try to break it down for him. "I want to take this slow."

He rears back. "Is this uncomfortable to you? We can go as slow as you want to. I don't want to pressure you."

I feel overheated. "No, it's not that." I blow out a breath and bury my forehead in his chest. "I'm a virgin," I mutter.

When he doesn't react, I raise my head and look at him through my hooded lashes. He doesn't look disgusted or as if he's about to run away. But he does look curious. "Did you just say you're a virgin?"

Embarrassment fills me. I roll my eyes. "Are you starting to think I'm more trouble than I'm worth?"

His voice is low and gruff. "Cass, baby, how could you think I'd be upset with that?"

I shrug. "I don't know. I'm sure you're expecting—"

He shakes his head and stops me. "I'm not expecting anything. You don't get it. I'm happy to just be here like this with you. I won't put any pressure on you. You have complete control of this, okay?"

I put my hand to his chest. "I said slow. I would still like to kiss you and just see where it goes."

He rolls to his back and pulls me on top of him. "You can kiss me anytime you want."

I say it before I can think twice about it. "What if I want more?"

His breath catches. "In case you haven't realized it yet, I won't tell you no. You want anything from me, you can have it."

I bite my lip. "Okay, so if I asked you to take your shirt off, you'd do it?"

His eyebrows lift in surprise. "You want me to take my shirt off?"

I nod. "Yeah, I do. Since I first saw you, I've wondered what you look like without your shirt."

He scoots to the side and pulls his shirt up his body, pulls it off his arms, and then tosses it on the coffee table. "There you go."

I'm staring at him, and I should probably make sure I don't start to drool. He's beautiful. The hard muscles of his abdomen are covered with a thin layer of dark hair that leads down and disappears under his pants. I can't stop myself. I reach out and brush my fingers across his chest.

He sucks in a breath, and I draw my hand back. "Oh God, Baker, I'm telling you I want to take it slow and I'm practically manhandling you. I'm sorry."

He grabs my hand and puts it back on his chest. "You can touch me if you want, Cass."

I trace the hard planes of his chest, and when I reach his nipple, I draw circles around it. He moans, and I stop. "Are you okay?"

He nods. "Yeah, it feels good."

I look at him curiously, and he asks, "Has anyone touched you there, Cass?"

I bite my lip and nod. "Yeah, but I didn't like it. He was squeezing me like I was an orange or something. It felt more weird than anything."

He opens his mouth and then closes it again. I can see the need in his eyes. "Baker... would you want to—"

He cuts me off. "Yes, fuck yeah, I want to touch you, but I don't want to pressure you."

I think about it for less than a second. I can't give up this opportunity. Who knows how long it will be before he comes to his senses? I lean up and grab the hem of my shirt, but he stops me. "Are you sure?"

I nod. "I trust you."

He helps me out of my shirt, and I try to reach behind me to unhook my bra. I finally get it and take it off, letting it fall to the floor. I'm nervous until I see the way Baker's looking at me as if I'm the most beautiful woman he's ever seen. "You're so perfect, Cass."

"I'm not, but you make me feel like I am."

His hand comes up and cups my breast. I'm not sure where it came from, but I moan and arch my back, pressing farther into his hand. His touch is soft but firm at the same time. When his finger caresses over my hard nipple, I feel like I could come right then. His voice is trembling. "Can I kiss you?"

I open my eyes and try not to freak out. "You want to kiss me… there?"

He nods, looking at me for approval.

I can't say no because right now I want his mouth on me more than anything. "Yes," I say throatily.

He doesn't hesitate. His lips seal over my nipple, and he suckles me. All at once, I feel him everywhere. His leg raises between my thighs, and he strokes me at my core. I feel wanton as I open my legs wider to let him slide his leg higher. With the friction between my thighs and his lips on my breasts, it becomes too much. I can feel the pressure rise. I clamp my legs together, squeezing his in a vise. My back arches even more, and I put my hand at the back of his head, holding him to me.

I've never had an orgasm with someone else in the room, but there's no holding back. I have no control over my body, and I can't fight it off. My whole body tenses and starts to jerk uncontrollably.

He doesn't stop. He keeps pleasuring my breast and rubbing his leg between my thighs. And I bask in my release until I have nothing left to give.

When I come down, embarrassment takes over. "Oh my God."

He's still nuzzling my breast, his head resting against me. His voice is thick. "You okay?"

I try to shift my body, and he groans. His manhood is hard and pressed against me. I ask him the same question. "Are you okay?"

He kisses my breast and then leans back to look at me. I start to apologize. "I'm so sorry—I don't know what came over me. I'm not—"

He stops me. "Don't ever apologize to me. I love seeing you like this."

I touch his shoulder. "But what about you? Do you want me to, uh, you know?"

"No. We'll get to that when you're ready."

I think back to my ex, and he was always pressuring me to do things. It's crazy because with Baker, I want to do those things, but he's willing to wait. Unsure where we go from here, I ask him, "So uh, now what?"

He leans his head against my naked breast. "I'd like to lay here, just like this for a while. We can talk, and I'll take you home… later."

I rest my chin against his head. "Sounds good."

Lying in his arms, I can't help but think about the future and wonder if there could be something between us.

CHAPTER 12
BAKER

AFTER TEXTING and talking on the phone all week, I finally get to have Cassie in my arms tonight. I only saw her once this week when I took her lunch at the school, but we've talked or texted all week long, multiple times a day. It has sucked not being able to hold her when I've seen her, but it's also been a good thing because we've talked and really got to know each other.

I turn my oven on warm and put the containers inside. I wasn't sure what Cassie would want to eat, so I ordered a little bit of everything. I'm pacing my living room when the doorbell rings.

I open the door, smiling ear to ear. "Hey, baby."

I instantly pull her into a hug, and her body melts against mine. I feel like I'm probably holding her too tightly, but I can't help it. I kiss the top of her head. "I missed you this week. Are you trying to kill me with this dress? You look beautiful."

She pulls away, and it's now I notice she's not happy. "What's wrong?"

She shakes her head. "I'm sorry, Baker."

"Sorry for what? What's going on?"

I gather her in my arms and pull her inside the house, closing the door behind us. "Talk to me. What's wrong?"

"Do you remember me telling you about my best friend, Haven?"

I nod. "The model, right?"

She rolls her eyes. "Of course you remember that part. Yes, the model. Anyway, she's in town for one night, and I haven't seen her in months. I may have to leave a little early and meet her in town or something."

"Invite her here."

Her eyebrows lift, and she points at the ceiling. "You want me to invite her here?"

I grab her hands and pull her farther into the house. "It will be perfect. I ordered way too much food, or heck if you want something else, I can order that. You can talk and not have to worry about the noise or anything. I'll go to my office and catch up on paperwork."

She tilts her head to the side. "Baker, I'm not going to invite my friend here and intrude on your space."

I wrap my arms around her and lock my hands together on her lower back. "You won't be intruding. I've been looking forward to this all week, and even if you're just in the other room, that's enough for me. I just want you here with me."

She wants to say yes. "Are you sure about this?"

"I'm positive. Call her. I'll set up the food at the table."

She pulls her phone out of her pocket. "Okay, if you're sure."

I lean down and kiss her. "I'm sure."

I walk into the kitchen, leaving her to make her call.

I'm setting the table when Cassie comes in. "She was a few minutes away."

I go to take the food out of the oven. "Perfect. I got a little bit of everything, so you can pick and choose."

"Thank you, Baker. Really, this is so incredibly nice of you. I really appreciate it. And I think you'll like Haven. Everyone does."

I carry some of the plates to the table, and she is following behind me with her hands full. "I'm sure I'll like her because she means something to you. Don't worry, okay?"

When the doorbell rings, I tell her, "Go ahead. You can get it. I'll finish here."

Cassie seems nervous all of a sudden, and so I figure she needs some time with her friend. I can hear them talking and once everything but the dessert is set out, I turn to face the living room.

Cassie is blushing when she gestures to me. "Haven, this is Baker. He's uh, my stepbrother. Baker, this is Haven. My very best friend in the whole world."

I try to hide my disappointment that she introduced me as her stepbrother. I'm not sure what I was hoping for, but I can't be upset. She said she wanted to keep our relationship between us.

Haven smiles and waves at me. "So your dad tamed the beast. I need to meet him sometime."

I look at Cassie, not sure if I should laugh or not, but she's smiling and shaking her head. "Yeah, Haven has met Brandi."

I nod. "Well, I'm sure my dad would love to meet you. He's really loving this being a girl dad. He'd be thrilled to meet Cassie's friends."

I gesture to the feast on the table. "I put out food, and you all should eat while it's warm. I'll be in my office if you need anything."

"Wait. You're not joining us? You have to eat," Cassie says. Of course she's worried about me.

I wave her off. "No, I want to give you two some time to catch up."

Cassie moves to block my path. "Absolutely not. Eat with us, then Haven and I can catch up."

I look between Haven and Cassie, and they're both nodding their heads. "Okay, sure. Let's eat."

I go grab another place setting and then wait for the women to sit. "Would you like water, soda, or wine?"

"Water," they say in unison.

I grab three bottles of water and carry them to the table.

I sit down, and the conversation is light as we talk about a little bit of everything.

Haven shrugs. "So we going to talk about Dick?"

I practically choke on my chicken Parmesan, and Cassie rolls her eyes. "Ignore her. She's talking about Richard, my ex." She turns to Haven. "There's nothing to talk about. I broke up with him." It's obvious that Cassie is trying to change the subject. "What's new with you?"

Haven looks at me before she answers, "Don't judge me."

I hold my hands up. "No judgment here."

I try to keep my head down and eat. I'm not sure what she's about to say, but after the dick comment, I feel like I should be ready.

"So you know the new therapist I've been going to, right?"

Cassie nods. "Yeah, you said you really like her and you can tell a difference since you started going to her."

Haven nods and eats a bite of salad. "Yeah, well, I did like her. She wants me to do something, and now

I think she's crazy. I don't know if I should just tell her no or find a new therapist or what."

Cassie lets her fork hover over her plate. "You've had three therapists in the last year. What does she want you to do?"

She blows out a breath. "She wants me to hire a cuddler."

Cassie rears back, and I know my eyebrows lift into my hairline. Cassie is shaking her head in confusion. "She wants you to hire a cuddler. What does that even mean?"

Haven looks at me, and it's obvious she's embarrassed. I act like I'm completely into the food I'm eating. "I guess since I have my 'issues,' she thinks that if I hired a cuddler I can work on stress, anxiety, and my boundary issues."

She looks at me again. "You didn't know Cassie's best friend was crazy, right?"

I laugh. "I don't think you're crazy."

Cassie's quiet and then blurts out, "You have to do it."

Haven looks at her in surprise. "Of everyone, I thought you'd agree with me. It's crazy."

Cassie is shaking her head. "It's not crazy. You know you have 'issues,' and I can see how this would help. They're professionals, right? It's not like you're just picking someone off the street or anything. It would be safe."

Haven doesn't seem so sure. "Yeah, I guess." She picks at her salad. "Let's talk about it later. What about you, Baker? What do you do?"

I answer her, and Haven is looking between us and then starts asking me one question after another. The more we talk, the more Cassie starts to look uncomfortable. The more Haven asks me questions, the quieter Cassie gets.

Cassie is looking between us, and she doesn't have to say anything for me to know what she's thinking. I should have known when she talked about Haven in the past and mentioned men always fall for Haven that I should tread lightly.

I lean forward. "So you're Cassie's best friend, right?"

Haven blinks and nods her head. "Yes."

I nod, hoping I'm doing the right thing. "So you want what's best for her?"

Haven looks at Cassie and then back to me. "Absolutely."

I nod and let out a breath. "Okay. Cassie and I are dating."

I know she wanted to keep us a secret, but she surely can trust her best friend. I look at Cassie, hoping she's not going to be mad at me, and I'm happy I said it because she's smiling ear to ear at me. She lights up. I reach out my hand for her, and she threads our fingers together.

Haven lets out an excited whoop. "I knew it. I knew it. Why didn't you tell me?"

I listen to the two of them talk, and Cassie is no longer unsure as she sits here. I don't know if she thought I would like her friend better than her or what, but somehow, I need to show her that I'll always choose her.

After we finish eating, I clear the table, insisting they stay where they're at.

I bring in dessert and set it in the middle of the table. Cassie gasps. "Is that the famous cinnamon Blaze cake from Red's?"

I nod. "It is."

I bring plates and utensils and set them on the table. I lean down and kiss Cassie on the lips. She blushes prettily, and I cup her chin. "I'm going to get some work done in my office. Just holler if you need anything. Haven, it was nice to meet you."

I walk out of the kitchen and barely get through the living room when I hear Haven loudly whisper, "Ooh, girl. He's got it bad. Tell me everything."

I can't help but smile. Haven's right. I have it bad.

CHAPTER 13
CASSIE

"Ooh, girl. He's got it bad. Tell me everything."

I'm watching Baker walk away, and I'm smiling as he goes. I'm not sure how he knew how I was feeling, but he caught on and wanted to reassure me the only way he thought he could. And it was perfect. Honestly, I would have eventually told Haven anyway.

I look at my best friend and am trying not to freak out. "He likes me, Haven."

She laughs. "He more than likes you. Did you see the way he was looking at you? I swear it got ten degrees hotter in here."

I slap her on the arm. "Stop. Let's talk about you. How's modeling going?"

She rolls her eyes. "It's fine. But I think I need to start thinking about retirement."

I gasp. "Retirement? You're twenty-five years old."

She nods knowingly. "I know that. I'm a plus size twenty-five-year-old model. It's about time."

"So what are you thinking about doing after?"

She shrugs. "I don't know."

"Don't lie to me, Haven. You have some idea what you want to do."

She doesn't look happy. "I know exactly what I want, but it will never happen."

"Tell me," I insist.

She takes a drink of her water. "Are you going to laugh?"

I roll my eyes at her. "I think you know me better than that. What is it?"

She starts to ramble. "I want to get married and have babies." She cringes and covers her face. "Did I just set women back fifty years or what? I sound so lame."

My mouth drops. I've known Haven a long time, and I've never heard her talk this way. "First of all, no you didn't just take us back fifty years. It's 2024! Women can have whatever we want. And you deserve that. You should do it."

She measures me with a look. "You know me. I can't get close to people, how do you expect that to work?"

I think about everything I know about Haven. I'm the first person that ever told her I loved her. She's never had affection in her life, and she's right. If she continues like she is, there's a small chance it will happen. I blurt out. "You should hire a cuddler. If that's what your therapist recommends, that's what you should do."

"Cassie," she starts, and I shake my head.

"No, Haven, hear me out. If that's what you want, you have to get to the point where you can accept intimacy. Do it."

She tilts her head to the side. "I'll think about it."

I nod and pat her on the shoulder and then draw back when she tenses up. "Sorry. Look, you'll figure it out. You're so smart and talented. And you're a hard worker. If you want something, you'll make it happen."

She shrugs, and I have to ask her, "Will you move back to Whiskey Run? Or stay in the city?"

"I really don't know."

I grab the plate of cake in the middle of the table and cut two pieces. I set one piece in front of her. "Here." She shakes her head, and I insist. "Haven, you ate chicken and lettuce with no dressing. Enjoy the cake."

She picks up the fork and takes a small bite then moans and smiles at me. "That's good."

I nod. "Yep, really good."

We spend the next couple of hours talking. When Baker comes out of his office, Haven stands up. "I really need to get out of here. I have a shoot in Jasper tomorrow afternoon."

Baker looks apologetic. "Don't leave on my account. I just needed to stretch my legs."

She shakes her head. "No, I really need to go. It was nice to meet you, Baker, and thank you so much for dinner and the cake. See you later, Cass."

We walk with her to the front door, and I call out to Haven as she walks down the steps, "I love you!"

She waves back, and we stand on the porch and watch her pull out. When we walk into the house,

Baker is smiling. "She's nice. She seems like a good friend."

I agree with him. "She's the best."

He wraps his arms around me. "So are you mad at me?"

I squeeze him around the waist in a big hug. "No, I'm not mad at you."

I pull at the hem of his shirt and pull it up his body. He lets me remove it, but I don't miss the surprised look on his face. As soon as I have my hands on his bare skin, I caress him, running my fingers across his nipples. He grabs my hand. "Cassie?"

I lean in, pressing my lips to his nipple, circling it with my tongue like he did to me. "Argh," he moans.

When I grab his belt and try to undo it, he grabs my hands and stops me. "Cassie, stop, what are you doing?"

I look at him through hooded eyes. "I'm sorry. I thought you wanted me."

He shakes his head. "You know I want you."

I laugh, hiding my insecurity. I pull away from him. "Forget it. I'm sorry, I just thought…"

I don't finish my thought. I'm not sure how to explain what I'm thinking, but after this week, I knew that I wanted to take our relationship to the next step. Baker is amazing. He's called and texted with me all week. He brought me lunch at school, and it was obvious he wanted to hug me and to kiss me, but he respected my wishes of keeping this secret.

"You thought what?" he asks me.

I shrug my shoulders as if it's no big deal. "Forget it. Let's watch a movie. That was the plan, right?"

I walk away from him and sit on the couch. When he doesn't follow me, I grab the remote and turn the television on. "What do you want to watch? Action, comedy… I think that new superhero movie is now streaming if you want to watch that."

He comes over and sits down next to me. He takes the remote from my hands and turns the television off. "Cassie, talk to me. What's going on in that pretty head of yours?"

I jut my chin at him. "Well, I thought we could, you know, but I guess not. It's not a big deal."

He tips my chin and searches my eyes. "You're saying you want to give me your virginity and it's not a big deal?"

I cross my arms over my chest. "You act like I'm some kind of slut or something. I'm not."

He puts a hand on each side of my neck. "Listen, okay? I want you. I've said it over and over, but this feels like a game to you. You want to keep this hidden—heck, you weren't even going to tell your best friend about us. You don't want anyone to know, and you said this is nothing serious. I don't want to make love to you and then have you walk away like it means nothing."

I choke back a sob. He's voicing all the worries I have for myself. I've thought the same thing about him. I've worried that if I slept with him, he'd walk away, but I told myself I had to trust him. "And you say I'm the one with the trust issues. What about you? You don't sound like you trust me at all."

His voice is pained. "Can I trust you? You've said over and over that this is not going to work."

I rear back as if he's slapped me. "Can you trust me? Of course you can trust me. I said that because I'm scared. I'm scared because I've never felt this way about anyone, and so yeah, I said I didn't want anything serious. I've even tried to convince myself of it, but it's too late. I like you, Baker. I like you a lot."

"Okay. I like you too… a lot. We don't have to rush anything. We can let it happen naturally."

I look at him curiously. "So you want it to happen?"

He grunts. "Cass… baby. I've stroked my cock, thinking of you every day this week. Yes, I want it to happen, but I want you to be sure. I'm not going to have sex with you and let you walk away from me."

The more he says, the more I know I'm making the right decision. I want Baker to be the one. I'm going to have to be bold, and that's not easy for me, but I have no doubt that he is worth it. "Okay, well, is it okay if I crash here tonight? I told Mom and Ryan that I was spending the night with Haven."

He points at the floor. "You want to stay here… all night?"

"Yeah, but I mean, I can sleep on the couch."

He bites his lip and looks at me with a dazed, glassy look in his eyes. "I have a spare bedroom. You can sleep in there if you want."

I try not to show my disappointment. "Great. Okay. I'm going to run out and get my bag out of the car."

I turn to go, and he grabs my hand. "You know you're not going to sleep in the spare room, right?"

I suck in a breath, hopeful. "Where am I going to sleep?"

"In my bed, next to me. Nothing has to happen, but I'm not letting this opportunity pass me by. I want to hold you all night."

My mouth falls open in an "Oh." He pulls me against him. "Is that okay with you?"

I nod. Satisfied, he points to the couch. "Have a seat. I'll get your bag."

He waits until I sit down before he grabs my keys on the entry table and then goes outside. When he comes in, he carries my bag down the hall, and I don't have to watch him to know he's taking it to his bedroom.

I get up from the couch and follow him. I'm surprised when I turn into the bedroom and he has one arm on the wall and is taking deep breaths. He looks like a man that is slowly losing control.

"What are you doing? You okay?" I ask him.

He raises his head and looks at me with a smoldering gaze. "I'm convincing myself I need to be strong."

I move, stepping under his arm and leaning back against the wall in front of him. "What if I want you to be weak?"

"Fuck, Cass, you don't know what you're asking me. I can't resist you."

I pull the dress I'm wearing up my hips slowly. When I get it to my chest, I pull it over my head and let it drop to the floor. As I'm standing here in front of him with only my bra and panties on, I get nervous. That is until I look into his eyes. The way he's looking at me is everything.

I undo my bra first and let it fall. Then I walk over to his bed, pulling the covers back. "I didn't bring pajamas. I hope that's okay."

He's speechless.

Before I get into the bed, I take a deep breath and then peel my panties down my hips and legs and kick them off my feet. I slide into the bed and pull the covers up over my body.

He's next to me in an instant. "You're in my bed, naked."

I laugh. "I know I am."

He starts to undress, and when he's down to his boxers, I hold my breath, waiting. His arousal is evident through the thin material, and I want to see all of him, but he doesn't remove the shorts. He walks around to the other side and climbs into the bed. He slides toward me until I can feel him hard next to me. He pulls me against him, and my whole body trembles on contact.

"You okay? I can hold you just like this, baby, and be satisfied."

He thinks I'm scared, and I thought I would be, but with him, I'm not. The desire for him has gone to a whole other level. That's all I'm thinking about. "I want to be with you, Baker. I want to be with you completely."

He groans and kisses me until I'm breathless. I hold on to him, smashing my breasts against his chest. Every fiber of me feels ignited as the hair-roughened length of his legs slide between mine. I feel him everywhere. His hands caress me, his lips are making promises that I hope he keeps. I break the kiss, arching my body into his. "It feels so good."

He pushes me to my back and gets on his knees, hovering over me. "You're so beautiful."

I don't normally take compliments well, but when he says it, I can see the truth of it in his eyes. He searches my eyes and leans over to kiss my lips. Then he trails kisses down my neck before suckling at my breasts. He grabs my legs, pushing them farther apart and then trails kisses down my stomach. My hands clench into the bedsheets as he gets farther south. My hips have a mind of their own and lift up, wanting to give him better access.

"Good girl," he murmurs in between kisses.

I didn't realize how much his approval would heighten my arousal.

He grabs a pillow, stuffing it under my hips, and then strokes his tongue along the seam of my core. My stomach muscles pull, and my head goes back.

Already it feels too good, and I'm not sure how I'm going to survive it.

CHAPTER 14
BAKER

I tried to do the right thing. I've told her over and over I'll wait, but there's only so much a man can resist. She says she's ready, so I have to trust what she says. All I can do now is make sure she doesn't ever regret it.

I lap at her, tasting her arousal. My cock is hard, leaking cum from my tip. I press my hips into the bed, hoping for any kind of relief.

Each pass of my tongue over her clit, she whimpers and jerks. She's so responsive to me, and I want to draw it out, but she's already soaked, coating my chin with her arousal. I pump one finger into her softly as I circle her clit with my tongue.

I listen to her, finding out what she likes and what makes her body buzz with anticipation. Her hand goes to the back of my head, and when her grip tightens, I know I'm hitting her just right. I apply more pressure, pump my finger a little deeper, and she starts to come. Her pussy floods, and she grips on to me like she never wants to let me go, so I give it all I've got. Her orgasm hits her hard and swift.

She jerks and writhes under me, but I don't relent. I keep lapping at her, tasting her fresh cum as it hits my tongue.

When she comes down, I slide up her body, ignoring my cock that's painfully hard. This is about her.

She's trying to catch her breath, and I pull her against me, holding her until she's settled.

"Baker?" she asks after a few minutes.

I kiss her forehead. "Yeah, baby?"

"What about you?"

I grunt because my cock is still hard as ever. "I'm fine. It will go away in a minute."

She lifts her head to look at me with her eyes wide. "But I don't want it to go away."

I shake my head. "I can't do it, Cassie."

She tries to pull away, but I don't let her. She doesn't understand. "No. Don't do that, listen to me. It's your first time, and I can't hurt you, Cass. I can't."

She searches my eyes, and her face lights up. I don't have to wonder long because she pushes me to my back. "Okay… can I be on top?"

She pulls my shorts down and then straddles me. My cock rests along her soaked pussy. I clench my eyes together. "Yeah, baby, you can be on top." I gesture with my head. "Come here."

She leans forward, and I kiss her, plunging my tongue into her mouth, sliding along her warm velvet tongue. She pulls away. "I can taste myself on you."

Fuck, my cock gets even harder. "Do I need to get a condom?" I ask her, wishing I could be in her bare. I shake my head quickly. "Fuck, yeah, let me get a condom."

I lift up, but she's pushing me back down. Her eyes are on me questioningly. "Do you want to wear one?"

I grit my teeth because I'm already imagining how good it will feel to be inside her. But above my own wants, I need to keep her safe. She's not ready for everything that comes with bare sex. But I'm honest with her. "No, I don't want to wear one. I'd love to feel your pussy vibrating around me, but you're not ready to tell anyone we're together, Cass. You're definitely not ready to be pregnant."

She bites her lip. "I'm on the pill."

My hips jerk. Fuck me.

"I'm clean," I tell her.

Her smile lights up the whole fuckin' room. "So no condom?"

I put my hands on each side of her face. "Are you sure about this?"

She nods and then tugs from my hold. She rises up and wraps her hand around my cock.

I put my hands on her hips and help her position herself over my cock. When I'm at her entrance, she slowly starts to sink down on me. With my hold on her, I'm fighting with myself to not draw her to me, impaling her on my cock.

She slowly starts to descend and stops.

"Breathe, baby. You're doing so good."

Her hands go to my chest, and she sinks lower. I can feel the sweat at my brow, and it's taking everything in me to not lift my hips. I know how good it's going to feel, but I need her to be okay.

When she hasn't moved, I brush her hair back from her face. "You okay?"

Instead of answering me, she looks me in the eye. "You ready?"

My jaw tightens. I don't know if I am or not, but I nod my head, and she impales herself on my cock. She sinks all the way down until I can feel her ass against my hips. I'm so deep and she's so snug I feel like I might faint.

There are tears in her eyes, and I reach up to wipe them away. "It's okay. Do you need to stop?"

She looks at me as if I'm crazy. "I'm going to move, Baker."

I nod, gritting my teeth.

She lifts up and lowers herself again, moaning along the way. Over and over, she lifts and lowers. She shifts her hips, trying different angles, and when she find what she likes, she starts to move.

"You okay?"

She answers with a moan.

I'm barely hanging on, but I need her to come with me. I reach between us and rub my finger along her already sensitive clit. Her thrusts become more erratic and her moans louder. "Oh, oh…"

I thrust up into her, and I know the exact moment her release comes. She bears down on me, and her pussy contracts, strangling my cock. She comes, and I shoot my seed deep inside her until I have nothing left to give.

She falls down on top of me. I could stay exactly like this the rest of the night, but I need to take care of her. For her first time, she's going to be sore. I turn us so she's on her side and then pull out of her slowly. She winces, and I reassure her with a kiss. "Stay right here. I'll be right back."

I get up and go to the bathroom, grab a washcloth, and run it under warm water. When I get back to her, she has a satisfied smile on her face, and I push her legs apart. Her hands go to cover herself, and I laugh. "Cass, I've had my face and my cock buried in your pussy. I think we're past the point of being shy don't you think?"

She lifts her hands, and I clean her gently. When I'm done, I lean down and kiss her. "Get up and take care of business, then we're going to shower."

Her eyes go wide. "Together?"

I lean in, unable to keep my mouth and hands off her. I kiss her and tell her, "I have you here until tomorrow. We're going to be doing everything together."

She nods, and I help her out of the bed and watch her walk into the bathroom. My cock already reacts to seeing her. I've never had this kind of a reaction to a woman before. Cassie is special, and I'm going to do everything in my power to make sure she knows it.

Tonight means more to me than she probably realizes. All I know is I've said it a few times, and now I mean it more than ever. She's mine. And I'm not letting her go.

CHAPTER 15
CASSIE

YESTERDAY I WENT HOME sore and satisfied. I ended up spending the whole day with Baker, and I felt a little guilty lying to Mom and Ryan when I got home. I think Ryan knew something was up, but he's too much of a gentleman to say anything. My mom doesn't have a clue what I do; she never did.

I got to school early this morning, and I'm waiting for the kids to get here while I go back though my text messages from last night and this morning. They're all from Baker, and I get butterflies in my stomach as I read them each again.

I read through our texts from last night first.

"When can I see you again?"

"We still haven't talked about the carnival."

He replied, "Tell me what kind of booth you want and I'll have it ready. I want to spend our time together a different way if you know what I mean."

I remember typing the next text without any hesitation. "I agree. I can think of better things we could be doing."

"Are you feeling okay?"

That was probably the tenth time he asked me that yesterday, and I answered him with a smile. "I'm perfect."

The bubbles had popped up immediately, letting me know he was writing something. "You are perfect."

But it doesn't stop there.

"All the way from that fiery red hair, to those sassy lips that I can't stop from kissing, that big soft heart, down to your curvy body that dreams are made of. Every bit of you is perfect, Cass."

I got a little choked up. The negative thoughts start to arise but I remind myself that Baker is not like any man I've ever known. He's not playing me. I typed out a text and sent it to him. "Tomorrow after school. I can see you then… and it won't be soon enough."

As I reread the texts, I'm hoping that today doesn't drag by.

Which of course it does. It's the slowest Monday I've ever had, but I've forced myself to keep my phone in my purse in my drawer so I'm not tempted to check it every five minutes to see if there's a new message from Baker.

Nothing exciting happened today, but at least all the kids were on their best behavior.

It's the end of the day, and I'm walking back from the office from making copies when Charlotte comes up beside me. "Did you hear about Colby Turner?"

I slam to a stop. "What happened?"

She grips my arm. "He left at lunch time, and no one has seen him since."

I think back to this morning when he was in my class. He was quiet, but he's always quiet. I try to remember anything about this morning that would have stood out, but I can't recall anything.

I talk to Charlotte for a few minutes and then I excuse myself to my room. I want to call Baker, that's the first thing I want to do, but I don't. All these feelings start to resurface, and I'm half afraid to call him. What if he's like every other person in my life, excluding my sister and Haven, and doesn't come when I need him? The fear of that happening is what stops me from calling him.

Plus, I'm sure Principal Daniels has notified the authorities, and he's already out looking for him. But I know I can't do anything.

I grab my purse and my tote bag of papers that need to be graded and walk to the front office. The secretary is still at her desk. "Have you heard anything about Colby?"

She shakes her head with a sad look on her face. "No, he's still missing."

I nod and walk out without another word. All I can think about is that I knew something wasn't right at Colby's home. I should have done more to help him. I've tried and tried to get him to talk to me, but he never did. I should have found a way.

I'm almost to my car when the police car pulls into the lot and comes to a stop next to me. Baker gets out, and I can't help it, the emotions rolling through me are so overwhelming I burst into tears.

He comes to me and wraps his arms around me. "Oh baby, it's okay. We're going to find him."

But even with his reassurance, I can't stop crying.

He's rubbing my back, saying soothing words in my ear, but I can't stop. I finally pull myself together when he says, "Baby, Colby needs you right now. I hate to see you upset. Please, trust me. We'll find him."

I suck in a sob and try to catch my breath. I've soaked Baker's shirt with my tears, but he doesn't seem to mind. He gathers my hair in his hands and pulls it off my shoulders, letting it fall down my back. "Talk to me. Why didn't you call me?"

I search his eyes and shrug. "I don't know."

He's not having it, though. "Cass, why didn't you call me?"

But I still don't answer him. He's frustrated, and I don't blame him. He blows out a breath and puts his arm around me as he walks me to his squad car. "Come on."

I stop before getting in. "Do you want me to follow you in my car?"

He shakes his head. "No, I want you to get in my car. I need to go find Colby, but I can't leave you when you're upset like this. Come on, you might know where he is."

I point to myself. "I might know? I don't have a clue. Have you talked to his mother?"

He sighs. "His mother was found passed out in her front yard. She almost od'd. She's been admitted to the hospital."

I gasp and bring my hand up to my mouth. "Oh no! Do you think Colby knows?"

He shrugs. "I'm not sure, but it's possible that she was strung out this morning before he went to school. Maybe something happened. We don't know for sure. I've called his uncle. He was in Jasper about to get on a plane but he's back in town and is searching for Colby too."

He sets me in his car, and instead of shutting the door, he squats next to me. "Think about it. You know Colby. What does he like to do?"

I wrack my brain trying to think of everything I know about Colby. "He loves to draw."

"We'll check the new art store in town."

I nod, thinking what a good idea that is. "He likes to read."

"The library. There's a hundred places he can hide in the library. What else?"

I try to think about it and lift my shoulders. I don't know if this is a good clue or not, but I'm willing to try anything. "This summer I met Chloe at the park to run the track there, and I saw Colby hanging out at the swings. I didn't know him then, but I noticed him because he was by himself, watching the ground as the swing swayed back and forth."

He claps me on the shoulder. "Good, good. We'll hit the art store, then the library, and if we still haven't found him, we'll go to the park. Good job, Cassie."

He kisses me, puts the seatbelt around me, and snaps it before closing my door.

I watch as he walks around to the driver's side of the car. Again, Baker has shown up for me when I needed him. I'm a fool if I don't start putting some faith in him.

CHAPTER 16
BAKER

I'M NOT sure how it's possible, but it is.

I'm fuming mad but I also want to hold her and make sure she's okay. Seeing her cry and break down the way she did had me wanting to throttle someone.

I can't handle her being upset, and the only thing I can think is I need to fix it.

I don't know why she didn't call me.

She gave herself to me, but she's still holding back, and I plan to find out why, but first I need to find the kid.

I drive across town, and she stays in the car as I run into the art store. I show the salesclerk Colby's picture on my phone, and she shakes her head. She allows me to search the store, and when he's nowhere to be found, I go back out to Cassie in the squad car.

We drive to the library next. "Come on. This place is huge. You can help me look."

She's going crazy sitting in the car, and it may help her if she's actively looking.

She walks with me into the library, and it takes everything I have not to hold her hand. When we get inside, I stop at the checkout counter and explain the situation. I turn to Cassie. "You take this floor and check everywhere. I'll take upstairs."

She nods her head, and I jog up the stairs. After fifteen minutes of searching, Colby is nowhere to be found. I stand at the top of the stairs and look down to the first floor, trying to see things from a different angle, but all I see is the desk clerk and Cassie going through the aisles searching.

I try not to let myself panic. Both places were such good ideas, and I don't know what I'm going to do if I can't find him. I promised Cassie I would.

I jog back down the steps and finish helping Cassie. After we're done, we go outside.

Cassie is not giving up. "Park next?"

I nod, and she gets in, snapping the seatbelt around her.

I drive us across town and stop at the parking lot to the park. This is pretty far from Colby's house and the school, but I'm still going to search it.

"You stay in the car on this one."

She's already undoing her belt. "Baker, I can go. I can help look."

I nod. "I know, but it's already starting to turn dusk. I'll go check around. You stay here. Please?"

She reluctantly nods her head, and I grab my flashlight out of the trunk and start walking to the park. I look everywhere along the walking path, the wooded areas to the side, and then I find myself at the swings.

I hear something and stop, holding my breath, hoping I'll hear it again.

"Officer Johnson?"

I let out the breath I'm holding and turn to the slide. There's a small tight spot underneath it, and I squat down and shine my light into it. The little boy's big blue eyes are staring back at me. "Hey, Colby."

He wraps his arms around his legs and stares at the ground. "You looking for me?"

I shine the light on the ground in front of him so it's not in his eyes. "A lot of people are looking for you. Miss Waters is in the car, and your uncle is worried about you. Half the town is looking for you right now, son."

He's quiet for a few seconds and then starts to stutter. "If I… I mean if I come out, are you going to make me go to my mom's house?"

I hold back the curse that I want to scream out. I can't imagine wanting to run away because of my mom. Times like this make me very thankful for the parents I had growing up. I hold my hand out to him. "No, you don't have to go to your mom's. We've sent her for help, Colby. Your uncle was hoping you'd want to come and stay with him."

He stays bent over as he climbs out from under the slide. "Are you serious, Officer Johnson? Can I stay with Uncle Raymond?"

I nod. I hope nothing has changed since I heard from the station earlier. "Yes, your uncle wants you with him while your mom gets help."

He comes the rest of the way out and stands up. He stands awkwardly, and I put my hand on his back. "You okay?"

He nods and stretches his legs out. "Yeah, I've just been under there for a while."

I pull my phone out. "I'm going to call the station and have your uncle meet us here, okay?"

I make the call and tell my sergeant that Colby is fine and where to find us. With one hand on his shoulder, we start walking out of the park. As soon as we get in sight of the squad car, the passenger door opens. "Colby!" Cassie hollers.

She starts running toward us, and I let go of the boy so he can meet her. She reaches for him, and they hug one another tightly. When I walk up on them, she's telling him that he can't ever run away again. "If you ever need help, you come to me, Colby. Or Officer Johnson. We both care about you, and we want to help you."

The boy starts blinking, and it's obvious he's barely holding it together. "My mom was up doing drugs all night. She was having a fit this morning when I left. I hate it when she's like that."

I bend down next to him. "We're sending her somewhere to get help."

He doesn't look convinced, and I know instantly what he's thinking. "And we won't let you go back to her if she doesn't get better."

The relief is evident as his shoulders drop and he takes a deep breath. "Okay."

The next few minutes are chaos. My sergeant shows up with Colby's Uncle Raymond. There are hugs and more tears, and when everyone gets in their cars to leave, I help Cassie back into mine.

She's pretty emotional, even now that the boy has been found. "You didn't know, Cass. You can't blame yourself."

She sniffs. "I know. Can you take me to my car? I feel a migraine coming on."

I start the car. "You have migraines?"

She nods. "Yeah, and I won't be able to drive once it gets worse."

She lays her head back on the seat. I pull out my phone and send a text to my sergeant. I've worked for the others plenty of times, and surely someone can cover my shift for me.

Without waiting for a response, I start driving to my house. She doesn't open her eyes the whole way. My phone dings when I'm almost home, and when I pull into the driveway, Cassie still doesn't open her eyes. I check my phone and read the text from my sergeant. "We got you covered."

I walk around to the passenger's side and open Cassie's door. She jerks awake and looks around in a daze. "Where… what are you doing, Baker?"

I talk softly to her. "I'm taking you inside."

I help her out of the car, and she leans her head against my chest. "But you have to work."

"I got someone to cover for me."

"Baker… you shouldn't miss work. If you take me home, I can lie down and I'll be fine."

I help her up the stairs and into the house. We bypass the living room, and I take her to my bedroom. After setting her on the bed, I help her take her shoes off. I grab one of my T-shirts and then take her silky shirt off and slide my shirt over her head and arms. I help her lie back, and then I take off her dress pants and then tuck her under the covers. I'm actually worried about how complacent she's being.

I lean over her. "What do you need?"

She tries to open her eyes and holds her hand over her face. "Can you turn the light off?"

I quickly shut the light off. "Okay, what else?"

"Can you get me some ice? Maybe some ibuprofen?"

"Done."

I walk softly back to the kitchen and grab everything I need. When I get back into the bedroom, she opens one eye to peek at me. She sounds so sad. "I'm so sorry, Baker. I haven't had a migraine in so long, but it usually happens when I cry. I have so much to do. I need to grade papers. If I can just rest a few minutes and get the medicine in me, I can get out of your hair."

I hand her the pills and help her sit up to take them. She takes a big drink of the water, and I set it on the nightstand. I grab the ice pack over my shoulder. "Lie back."

She lies back, and I lay the ice pack gently across her head.

She gasps, and I ask her, "Is that okay?"

She moans. "It's heaven."

"Lie back and rest. I'll be back soon."

"Where are you going?"

"I'm going to get your car from the school."

She doesn't argue with me, which tells me how bad she's feeling. I tiptoe out of the room and then grab my phone. "Dad, you busy?"

Cassie is not going to be happy with me, but I don't have a lot of choices. And I trust my dad more than anyone.

I drive over to my dad's, and he's waiting outside when I pull in.

He tosses a bag into the backseat. "Son, what are you doing?"

I explain everything about Colby and how Cassie was upset and had a migraine. It takes only minutes to get to the school, and I hand my dad the keys. When he gets out, he asks, "Now where am I taking her car to?"

I jut my chin at him, hoping he doesn't challenge me. "My house. She's going to stay there until she's feeling better."

His voice hardens. "Are you sure about this?"

Confidently, I nod my head.

He sighs and goes to get in Cassie's car. He follows me to my house. After parking, he comes and gets in my car, handing me her keys. "How come I feel like I'm on some secret mission or something?"

I swallow. "Dad, I'm not asking you to lie to your wife…"

I let my voice trail off. Cassie doesn't want our family to know, but there's no doubt my dad knew how I felt that first night. I don't care who knows, but I also don't want Brandi causing problems with her daughter.

"I packed clothes and stuff. It's all in her bag." He sighs. "I won't have to lie. Brandi was caught up in something on TV. She probably won't even know I'm gone."

"I'm sorry, Dad."

I don't know if he realizes I'm not only apologizing that I'm sort of asking him to lie but also that he has a wife that pays him no attention.

"It will all work out, son. It's okay."

We get back to his house, and he climbs out. "Take care of Cassie and let me know if I need to do anything for her."

"Will do, Dad. Thank you." Because I'm still feeling the effects of earlier and everything with Colby, I continue, "And thank you for being the best dad. You have always been here for me, and I just want you to know I love you. I want you to be happy, Dad."

He seems surprised, which reminds me that I don't tell him I love him enough. He finally nods. "I love you too, son."

He stands back from the car and walks toward the house as I pull out. When I get back home, I carry in Cassie's purse, school tote bag, and the bag that my dad packed.

I check on Cassie, take a quick shower, and then sit down to grade some middle school papers.

Almost three hours later, I'm about to lose my mind. Who would have thought middle school math would have changed as much as it has since I was in school? I aced 8th grade math, and tonight I had to search online how to solve some of the problems just so I could do a grading sheet. After I have the grade key, I work through the papers quickly. I'm so engrossed in them I don't hear Cassie until she's standing over me.

"What are you doing?"

She's looking between me and the stacks of papers. I stand up and move some of them off the couch so she can sit down. She sits next to me, and the T-shirt she's wearing rides up her thighs. The need to touch her is overwhelming, but I satisfy it by holding her hand. "Here. Sit. Can I get you anything?"

She shakes her head, still in awe. "Are you grading my papers?"

I nod. "Yeah, I knew you were worried about it, so I thought I could help. I had no idea that math was this hard, though, I'll tell you that. Are you feeling better?"

A thoughtful smile curves her lips. "A lot better. I can't believe you're doing this…"

I caress my fingers along hers. "You can't believe that I want to take care of you and help you?"

She must remember our discussion from earlier because her smile slowly disappears. "You asked me something earlier, and I didn't answer you."

I nod, waiting for her to tell me now. She squeezes my hand. "Don't be mad at me."

I fit her hand between both of mine. "In case you haven't figured it out, you're impossible to stay mad at."

She takes in an unsteady breath. "I didn't call you about Colby earlier because I was afraid you wouldn't come."

Floored, I don't completely understand. "What do you mean you didn't think I'd come?"

She blinks up at me. "I'll be honest with you. When I found out about Colby running away, you were the first person I wanted to call…"

I wait for her to continue and she finally takes a deep breath and goes on. "People don't show up, Baker. Trust me, I know this better than anyone. I didn't want to call you and be let down."

I try not to be angry, but it's hard that after everything she still doesn't trust me. "Cassie, you don't get it. I want to be the person you lean on. I want you to call me. I want you to know I'll be there for you. You need me, no matter what I have going on, I'll be here for you."

She shakes her head. "I'm sorry, Baker. I really am."

I pull her against me in frustration. "Stop. Don't apologize. I know when you've been let down so many times it's hard to believe, but I won't let you down. You just have to let me in."

She nods and buries her head in my chest. "Did I hear you say you got my car earlier?"

I tense, and she notices. She pulls back to look at me, and I can't lie to her. "Okay, so my turn. Don't be mad."

She bites her lip. "What did you do?"

I figure the best way to do this is to get it all out in the open. "I asked my dad to pack you a bag." I point at her bag across the room. "And he rode with me to get your car."

She gasps and shakes her head. "But… what… oh my, Baker what did you do?"

"I am not sorry, Cass. Right now, he thinks I'm taking care of you… that's all."

"My mom will make my life a living hell."

I wince. "I think my dad knows that because he's the most honest man I know and he didn't tell Brandi where he was going."

She shakes her head. "What are we doing, Baker?"

I stack up all her papers and lift her up from the couch. Grabbing on to her thighs, I pick her up, and her legs go around my waist. "I'm too big for you to carry."

I walk with her in my arms down the hallway, "I've told you once and I'll tell you again. You're perfect."

I lay her back on the bed and then strip down. She watches me closely as I slide into the bed, pulling the covers up over us. She curls into me, and her hand starts to slide down my chest. I grab it and hold it over my heart. "Not tonight. I want to, don't get me wrong, but you need to rest."

"Baker…"

I cut her off. "I told you I want to take care of you. Let me."

She leans against me, and I hold her in my arms until she falls asleep. I lie awake, wondering how I can have her by my side just like this for the rest of my life.

CHAPTER 17
CASSIE

I woke up this morning in Baker's bed.

I didn't want to go to school, but I knew I should be there for Colby if he was there, so I got myself ready, smiled at the graded papers that were put back in my tote, and then kissed a sleeping Baker goodbye.

The day was uneventful if you don't count my sister and Chloe both texting me insisting on girls' night tonight. I don't really feel up to it, and I'd rather go spend time with Baker, but I also know that I might need to talk to my sister and my friend about everything that's going on.

So here I am at the Whiskey Whistler again, hoping not to get another repeat of the last time I was here.

With Chloe watching Elias in the corner, I turn to my sister. "How did the interview go?"

She takes a drink of her Margarita. "Surprisingly good."

I roll my hand at her, needing more information. "And? What happened? Did you get the job?"

She nods. "I got a job... but not the job I was applying for."

"What do you mean?"

She takes another big sip of her drink. Brook is happy, and I'm happy for her. She wants to get her own place, and this job could help her do it even sooner.

She leans forward. "Get this. Are you ready? I don't know if you're ready."

"What?" I ask her.

She leans in. "I'm going to be Walker's assistant. His personal assistant."

I rear back in shock. "Uh... what... how did that happen?"

She lowers her voice and leans in. "I seriously have no fuckin' clue. I went in and applied for one job, and they gave me another."

She throws her hands up. "Cassie, I get health insurance, a big sign-on bonus, matching 401k, and a company car."

I laugh in shock. "Are you kidding me? Brook, that's amazing! I'm so proud of you."

She nods. "I know, right? I'm pretty damn proud of myself."

Chloe leans in. "I personally don't know how you'll do it. Walker is hot. Capital H O T."

Brook fans herself, and I don't even think she realizes she's doing it. "Okay, enough about me. What about you? Why are you glowing?"

I instantly go on the defense. "Glowing? I'm not glowing. What are you talking about?"

Chloe leans in. "You're definitely glowing."

I guess the best defense is to go on offense. "So what happened the other night with you and Elias?"

She blushes. "Nothing. He's leaving soon to go on tour to the Middle East."

I grab on to Chloe's hand. "Oh, Chloe. I'm so sorry. I see the way you two look at each other. That sucks. Maybe when he gets back…"

I let my voice trail off because she's already shaking her head. "No, he said he'd probably be gone for two years. Maybe more."

"Damn, that sucks. I'm sorry."

She shrugs, trying to act as if it doesn't bother her, but I can see that her heart is breaking. I look across the room at Elias, and he has the same forlorn look as Chloe. I have to believe that something will happen there.

Chloe brings me from my thoughts. "Uh-oh, the cops are here again. Are they going to need to break up another fight, Cassie?"

I can feel my whole body heat. I don't even have to turn around to know that Baker has walked into the building. It's like my body is on high alert when it comes to anything to do with him. Brook turns to the entrance. "Oh, it's Baker."

My mouth drops. "You know Baker?"

She looks at me as if I have three heads. "Uh, he is our stepbrother."

Chloe gives me a knowing look. "Yeah, Cassie, he is your stepbrother."

As he gets closer, Brook opens her arms. "Hey, big brother."

I watch them hug, and it kills me. I know it's innocent, but I still don't like it.

When they pull apart, Baker's eyes meet mine. "Hey, Chloe." His voice softens. "Hey, Cassie."

I force a smile to my face. "Hey, Baker."

Brook is unaware of anything happening and smacks Baker on the arm. "Guess what? I got the job!"

He holds his fist out for her to bump. "Awesome. I knew you would! Congratulations! So what does this job entail exactly?"

She pauses for effect. "I'm going to be Walker's assistant."

"Wow! That's pretty impressive. Good job, sis."

I cringe when he calls her sis.

A man comes up, and Brook knows him. They talk for a second, and then she gets up. "I'm going to dance. I'll be back."

She disappears in the crowd, and I look at Chloe. She holds her hands up. "I uh, need to go to the bathroom."

I shake my head. "You just came back from the bathroom."

She gets up anyway. "Yeah, well, I need to make a phone call."

She looks between Baker and me and gives us a thumbs-up before disappearing in the crowd.

Baker comes to stand next to me. "I hate this."

I smile and wave at one of the moms from school as she passes by. "Hate what?"

"I want to touch you, Cass. I want to kiss you and let everyone here know you're taken."

I bite my lip at the images he provokes. I don't have to answer him because he changes the subject. "I hear Colby was at school today. Did he seem okay with everything?"

I turn, surprised that he asked about him. "Yeah, he actually seemed really good. His hair was combed, his clothes were clean. He brought a lunch to school, and he participated in class. I'd say today was really good for him."

He lets out a breath, and I realize he'd been worrying about him. For the first time since he walked in, I make eye contact with him. "I'm sorry, Baker. If I'd known you were worried, I would have called you and told you he was doing good."

He shrugs. "I went by the school and talked to Mrs. Daniels. She told me he was there and seemed fine."

I don't try to hide my surprise. "You came to the school today?"

He nods.

I tilt my head. "You didn't come see me."

He rubs at the scruff of his chin. "I wanted to, but I didn't think you'd want me to. I wasn't sure what to tell them to get down to your classroom. That day I brought you lunch, I got the tenth degree of questions." He sighs and almost sounds angry. "I know how important it is for you to keep this hidden."

"Baker, that's not fair."

He leans in, and I can feel this breath on my cheek. "No, what's not fair is I had my tongue in your pussy the other night and now I can't even touch you. That's not fair."

CHAPTER 18
BAKER

As soon as I walked into the bar, my cock was hard for her. Standing here, this close to her and unable to touch her is pure hell.

Her eyes are dilated, nostrils flared, and the pulse at her neck is vibrating. At least she's affected by me, that much is obvious. But her words say otherwise. "Baker, we've been through this. We can't."

"Fuck that. We can. We're grown-ups."

She slaps her hand on the table and then loudly whispers to me, "Think about your dad. Somehow, I'm not sure how, but he's happy with my mom. Do we want to be the ones to screw it up for them?"

"It won't screw with them. You know my dad. He loves me and above anything else, he wants me happy. He loves you too, Cassie. He wants you happy. He would never begrudge us happiness."

Chloe comes back to the table, takes one look at us with raised eyebrows, and shakes her head. "Uh, I'll go make another phone call."

Cassie turns on me. "Can we talk about this some other time? Please, Baker. Don't do this now. Not here."

I hang my head and grit my teeth. "Fine. I need to go check on things anyway. You okay here?"

For the first time since I walked in, she smiles. "Yeah, I promise no more bar fights." She points at her glass. "And I'm drinking water."

I'm about to go when I stop. I lean down and whisper in her ear, "Are you going to dance with anyone while you're here?"

There's a softness in her voice when she answers me, and it reminds me of the times we've been in bed together. "You mean with a man?"

I growl. It comes out before I can stop it, and she's lucky I don't throw her over my shoulder and carry her out of here in front of half the damn town. "Yeah, Cassie. Are you going to dance with a man?"

"No." She lifts her big green eyes at me, and I see the sincerity in them. "The only man I want to dance with is you. No one else."

I let my hand find her leg under the table and squeeze. "One day, Cassie, I'm going to dance with you in front of everyone. Our family, our friends, everyone. We're not going to care who sees us because you're going to trust in me and what we have together."

I see the question in her eyes, but I know she's not going to put voice to it. She's not going to ask me here in front of everyone. I wish she would because I'm dying to tell her exactly how I feel about her. But she's not ready. And there's a part of me that wonders if she ever will be. "I'll talk to you later, Cass. Call me if you need me."

She gives me one firm nod. "I will. Be safe out there, Baker."

I'm about to go when she stops me. "Are you coming to dinner on Sunday night?"

I shake my head, letting her know I don't know anything about it.

"Mom planned dinner for Sunday night. She said she mentioned it to you. Did she not?"

I stare at her without blinking. It's a slippery slope, but I don't want to diss her mom to her. The fact is Brandi doesn't want me around. She doesn't want to share my dad with anyone. My guess is she's seen how much my dad cares for Cassie, and that's why she wants her out of the house too.

There's a part of me that wants to say no. It's pure torture being this close to her and not being able to touch her. But I also know that any chance I have to be with her, I'm going to take it. Instead of answering her question about her mom, I ask, "What time?"

"Six o'clock."

Her green eyes search my brown ones, and I know I can't say no. "I'll be there."

I nod my head and walk away. I'm tired of doing it because when it comes to Cassie, I just want to stay.

My shift goes incredibly slowly. I drove by the Whistler a few times, and when my shift is over, I drive by there one more time. Cassie is leaving the parking lot so I follow her through town, parking on the road down from my dad's house. I should leave her alone, but I hate that we sort of argued. I keep pressuring her, and maybe I shouldn't. Maybe I just need to wait until she makes the decision on her own.

So I climb up the tree next to her window and with a soft thud, jump onto her balcony. Not wanting to scare her, I text her. "Hey."

She answers immediately. "Hey. I was hoping I'd hear from you. I'm sorry about tonight."

Awww, this girl is killing me. She's so good for me. "Open your balcony door."

It takes her only a minute, and she opens the door, looking at me in shock. "Baker, what are you doing here?" She practically throws herself into my arms. "I'm so sorry about tonight. I know it's hard. It was hard for me too. One of the things I love about you is how you're always touching me, and it kills me when we can't touch each other."

I want to argue with her and tell her that we could. All we need to do is come clean, but I don't want to have a disagreement with her right now. She leans up on her tiptoes. "Are you going to kiss me or what?"

She doesn't have to ask me twice. I walk her into the room and kiss her along the way. She pulls me down to her bed, and I hover over her. I can't get enough of her. I feel like I'm looking at her with my heart in my eyes, but I don't try to conceal how I feel about her. I wasn't lying to her because I want the whole town to know.

She lifts her hip. "Is that a gun or are you happy to see me?"

I raise up and remove my holster and belt and lay it on the floor next to the bed before lying back down. I push my hips into her. "That's for you."

We kiss some more, and I roll, bringing her on top of me.

She's searching my eyes, and I can see she has something on her mind. "How's your head?"

She nods. "Good."

I kiss her forehead. "What's on your mind?"

"Can I ask you something without you getting mad?"

I pull her down slowly because I like having the weight of her on me. "You can ask me anything."

She's looking at my chest now instead of my eyes. "I was talking to your dad…"

Her voice trails off, and I nudge her to look at me. "Tell me… it's okay."

"He mentioned Gina."

I wait for her to continue. "What about her?"

She's drawing circles on my chest through my shirt. "Your dad said you were crazy about her."

I run my hands through her hair, tangling my fingers in the silky strands. "Did he tell you she cheated on me? That she didn't want anything serious and was playing me?"

"She sounds stupid."

I laugh. "Yeah, well, thanks for that."

When she doesn't say anything else, I tilt her head up to look at me. "What are you thinking?"

She bites her lip. "Uh, well, I was just wondering if you still love her."

I'm staring at her, and she looks away. I bring her to the side of me and wrap an arm and leg around her, pulling her against my body. "Look at me."

She raises her big green eyes at me, and I can see the vulnerability in them. "Two things you need to know about me. If I loved another woman, I wouldn't have made love with you the other night. That's not who I am. Second, since the night I walked in the Whistler and saw you holding that ice pack to your head, I haven't even thought about another woman but you."

She slides her hand around my waist, holding on to me. "You don't have to say that—"

I cut her off. "Say what? That I want to spend time with you? That I want you? That all I can think about is you? Talking to you, laughing with you, being inside you…"

She challenges me with a look. "Show me…"

"Here?"

She pulls away from me and stands up. I watch as she undresses, and she's hiding nothing from me. "I want you too, Baker."

She's standing out of reach, so I get off the bed and come for her, but she holds her hand up to stop me. She points at my uniform. "Clothes off."

I make quick work of removing my clothes, and when I'm naked, she's licking her lips, staring at my erect manhood. I wrap my hand around my girth and stroke it twice.

Her eyes are glassy as she looks at me. "It kills me that I couldn't touch you earlier."

I stroke myself again, but it's not enough. With a husky voice, I tell her, "You can touch me anytime you want."

She puts her hands on her hips. "What if I want to do something new?"

I shrug. "As long as it ends with me inside you, you can do whatever you want."

She looks at her closed bedroom door and back at me. "You going to be able to be quiet?"

I laugh, because we both know she's the loud one. "Are you?"

She grabs a pillow off the bed and drops it to the floor in front of me. As she lowers to her knees in front of me, my body starts to tremble. I cup the side of her cheek. "You know you don't have to do this."

She reaches up, wrapping her hand around my length and smiles. "I want to."

My hips jerk as she holds me. She takes her time caressing me. Her strokes are soft yet firm. When she leans forward and presses her lips to the tip of my dick, I know I'm not going to be able to take much. Her first kiss is sweet and timid. I gather her hair away from her face and hold it in my hand as she licks me.

Her tongue strokes the underside of my cock from root to tip, and there's no stopping my hips from plunging forward. When she takes me in her sweet mouth, it's pure torture.

She's bobbing her head, and my head falls back as I groan.

She slaps my leg and pops off me. "Ssshhh," she reminds me before wrapping her lips back around my cock. When her hands go to my ass, holding me to her as she takes me, I know that I'm going to lose it. As good as this feels, I want to be inside her.

I grab her under arms, and she releases me. I pick her up and carry her to the bed and lay her back. Her red hair is spread out around her head, and her lips are wet and swollen. She's so beautiful, I would be happy looking at her just like this for the rest of my life.

I reach down and run my fingers through her slippery folds. Her arousal coats my fingers, and I lean down to kiss her. "You liked sucking me, didn't you?"

She murmurs her agreement against my lips. I pull her hips to the edge of the bed and position my cock at her entrance. Slowly, I enter her, and with one thrust, I bury my cock so deep inside her I'm not sure where I end and where she begins. Her pussy contracts at the intrusion, and I wait for her to adjust to me. When she starts to wiggle underneath me, I know she's ready and wanting more.

She fits me like a glove. "I want to fuck you like you're mine, Cassie."

She arches against me. "I am yours."

I put a thumb at her swollen clit and rub it back and forth as I move in and out of her. She's clenching on to me, and when she moans, I lean over to kiss her, quieting the sounds. The kiss is intense and adds to my arousal.

"Come for me, Cassie. I need you to come, baby."

Her fingers dig into my chest as I pummel into her. When the orgasm shoots through her body, she clamps down on me, and we come together. It takes everything inside me to bite my tongue and not tell her that I'm falling in love with her. But then again, how can she not know already? The way we are together… she has to know.

CHAPTER 19
CASSIE

"I can't believe I let you talk me into this."

My sister is sitting on the couch, surveying the room as if a bomb is about to go off. Which I guess is plausible if Mom is anywhere around. But still, my sister is exaggerating a little bit. "It's a family dinner with Mom and her husband. It's not like I asked you to donate a kidney or anything."

She barks out a laugh. "Really? I think donating a kidney would be easier and I guarantee more fun."

"There you guys are," my stepdad says as he walks into the living room. "You hiding out?"

I point to the kitchen. "Mom said she didn't want us in the kitchen, so you're stuck with us."

He laughs. "Well, it's my lucky day. You know I always wanted a girl. I mean nothing against Baker. He's a great son, but I always thought I'd be a good girl dad too. Now I have two daughters."

I stand up and hug him. "You are the best girl dad." And I'm not lying. I would have given anything to have had a father like him when I was growing up.

My sister follows suit and hugs Ryan too. She doesn't talk about the past much, but it's obvious she appreciates our newest stepdad. He has sort of become our calm in the chaos.

The doorbell rings, and I try not to act too excited, but both my dad and sister look at me strangely when I announce, "I'll get it."

I practically skip to the door, a big smile pasted to my face. But when I open it, I'm taken aback, and it feels as if I've been hit in the gut. "Richard, what are you doing here?"

He smiles as if I didn't catch him having sex with some girl at his apartment. "Didn't your mom tell you she invited me to dinner?"

I practically choke on the words. "You're not eating dinner here."

"Cassie Waters!" my mom admonishes me. "I raised you with better manners. Let the man in."

He walks in, and I move as far back as possible because I don't want him to touch me. I follow behind him into the living room, and my sister says. "What the fuck are you doing here?"

For the first time in ever, Richard doesn't sound as cocky as he usually does. "Brandi invited me."

My stepdad stands up. "What's going on? Who is this?"

Brook comes to stand between Richard and me. "That's Richard, Cassie's ex-boyfriend. And he's a dick."

Mom raises her hands up. "Now, girls, this is my house and you can't be rude to my guests. Ryan, pour Richard a drink. I need fifteen more minutes and we can eat. Girls, behave."

All I can do is stand here dumbfounded. How can my mom think this is okay? This isn't her trying to set me up. This is her trying to get back at me for something.

The front door opens, and Baker walks in.

Ryan looks relieved to see him. "Good. Hey, son, glad you're here."

He's smiling when he looks at me, but when he sees my face, his smile drops. "What's wrong?"

He looks around the room. "What the—"

I grab his arm and start to tug him from the room. "Baker, I have a shelf in my room that I need help putting together. Can you help me?"

I don't even look at the other three in the room. I just keep pulling until Baker follows me up the steps. As soon as we're in my bedroom, I shut the door and lean my head against his chest.

His arms go around me instantly. "What the hell is going on, Cass? Why is your ex-boyfriend here?"

I'm quick to assure him, "I didn't invite him. My mom did."

"Fuck." He grunts. "Fine. I'll get rid of him."

I shake my head. I'm so overwhelmed right now, and I just don't get how a mom could do something like this to her daughter. "I tried. My mom did the whole *my house, my rules.*"

He wraps his hands around my upper arm and leans back so he can look me in the face. "Fine. We'll leave then."

He's about to walk out my door when I stop him. Geez, this is a mess. "Wait. Listen. Your dad has talked about how excited he was to have the three of us under one roof. He's been looking forward to it all week."

"My dad would not want you to sit there with a man that hurt you. He wouldn't. Now this is crazy, Cassie. We're leaving."

I don't budge, though. "I'm not leaving. I won't hurt your dad. I won't do it. Let's just get through this... for your dad."

He doesn't want to. I can tell he's pissed, and I can't blame him. There's no way I'd want to sit down at a dinner table with his ex, Gina. No, this is a mess, but Ryan doesn't deserve for us all just to bail on him. If I leave, Baker leaves. If I leave, Brook will leave. Family dinner will be royally screwed.

Baker's jaw is pulled so tight, I'm waiting for it to crack. "If he touches you—"

I shake my head. "He won't."

"If he disrespects you—"

I assure him. "He won't." Geez, I hope he doesn't because I can see Ryan and Baker fighting with him today. "He won't," I say again because I'm trying to convince myself.

I'm about to walk out of the room when Baker stops me. "Why are you so calm about this?"

I don't know what to tell him. He doesn't have any clue the shit Brandi subjected Brook and me to growing up. There were parts of my childhood that were pure hell. And it sucks, but this little stunt my mom pulled today is nothing compared to some of her actions in the past.

I guess I'm quiet for too long because he asks me with concern on his face, "Are you having second thoughts?"

"Second thoughts?" I ask in confusion. "You think I'm having second thoughts about you?"

He shakes his head with a huff. "Well, I didn't think that, but are you? I mean, I was asking if you're having second thoughts about Dick."

CHAPTER 20
BAKER

I WAIT NERVOUSLY for her to answer. I'm holding my breath wondering what the hell I'll do if she says yes. I can't walk away from her, and I won't give her up. There's no chance.

Her eyes get big, and she's shaking her head. "Second thoughts about Dick? No, Baker. I'm not having second thoughts about him. I felt nothing when I saw him. Nothing."

Her hands go up my chest, and she wraps her arms around my neck. "You said you haven't looked at another woman; well, the same goes for me. I haven't looked at another man."

She leans up on her tiptoes and kisses me lightly. "Come on. We better get down there."

I hold on to her, not ready to let her go. "Hey, talk to me. Are you okay? This shit with your mom…"

I let my voice trail off because Brandi is still her mother. I shouldn't talk shit about her, but at some point Cassie is going to have to stand up to her.

She blows out a breath. "Yeah, I'm okay. I don't want to go down there, but I know I need to. I wish I could stay up here with you and have a repeat of the other night." She peers over at her bed, and I know she's remembering the same thing I am.

I lean my forehead against hers. "I wish…"

When I stop, she leans her head back to look in my eyes. "What? You wish what?"

"Forget it… it's sick and twisted, and it's my own issue."

Her curiosity is piqued. "What is it, Baker. What do you wish?"

I reach down between us. Cassie is wearing a skirt and I slide my hands up her thighs and cup her sex. "I wish my cum was seeping out of you when we go down there—"

She gasps, and I stop. "I know. See, I told you it was sick and twisted. I just need to claim you, Cass. I need to know when we go down there, you're mine. I want you to feel my seed leaking between your legs. I want your cream all over my dick as I sit across the table from him." I blow out an aggravated breath. "You're mine, Cass."

Her eyes light up, and she reaches for my belt buckle. "Do it. I want that too."

She undoes my belt and pants, shoves them to my thighs, and then raises her skirt up. She barely gets her panties off and I have her bent over the bed, ass in the air, and I impale her on my cock. She takes me easily because I'm finding that Cassie is always ready for me.

I thrust into her, and she moans. She turns her head into the bed to silence her noises, but I thrust harder. Fuck, I want them all to hear me satisfy her. I'm like a beast unleashed as I pound into her. Her back arches, and she slams her body back into me with each thrust. I reach around, and I barely touch her swollen clit before I feel her spasm around me. We come, and I don't stop until I've painted her insides with my cum.

It was quick and dirty, but I think it's what both of us needed.

I pull out of her and help her stand up. Her hair is everywhere. Her makeup is smudged, but she's smiling with satisfaction. I smooth her hair down, and then I grab her panties and she steps into them. Before I cover her pussy, I pierce her with my finger and then paint her pussy and thighs with my spunk that is trying to escape. "Mine," I tell her.

She doesn't complain. As she pulls down her skirt, I look down at my cock, covered in her sweet honey. I pull up my underwear and pants and buckle my belt.

She's watching me, and the possessiveness I feel for her takes over. "You look like you were just fucked."

I expect her to admonish me or freak out, but she doesn't. I lift my shirt and use it to wipe the mascara from her eyes. "You ready?"

She nods, and I can't resist. I kiss her like my life depends on it, and when her lips are nice and swollen, I grab her hand. "Let's go."

Cassie's face is red as we descend the stairs. Before we get into sight, I bring our hands up, kiss her fingers, and then reluctantly let her hand go.

When we walk into the living room, my dad is looking at me with raised eyebrows. Dick is sitting on the couch looking disgruntled, and Brook bounds out of her seat and comes for Cassie. I hear her whisper, "It's like that, is it?"

Cassie turns a deeper shade of red, and I puff my chest out. There's absolutely no shame coming from me.

Brandi walks in and claps her hands together, completely clueless to the climate in the room. "All right, everyone. Dinner's ready." She turns to me. "What are you doing here?"

I open my mouth, but Cassie beats me to it. "I invited him to OUR family dinner, Brandi."

I nod as Brandi grits her teeth. "Well, I'll grab another place setting."

We all go into the dining room, and I physically put Cassie into a seat and then sit right next to her. Brook sits across the table. Dad sits in his normal seat, and Dick is left standing at the lone seat without a place setting.

Brandi is all huffy as she comes in, seeing what we all did, but I could give two fucks. If she wants to be hospitable to the guy, that's on her. No one else will.

As the dishes start to get passed around, there's an awkward silence that settles around the table. Cassie leans forward. "Brook, did you tell Mom and Ryan about your new job?"

She was so excited about it the other day, but now she's very melancholy about the whole thing. "Yeah, I got the job."

Brandi turns her nose up. "At the bar?"

Brook rolls her eyes. "No, actually I'll be working for Walker as his assistant."

When Brook mentions Walker, one of the most powerful men in Whiskey Run, she perks up. "The Walker?"

Richard pipes up. "I'm looking for a new job. I wonder if he's hiring."

And just like that, awkward silence ensues. I stab at the meat on my plate and take a bite even though I've completely lost my appetite. The man sitting across from me disrespected Cassie, and I can't let him get away with it. "What do you drive, Dick?"

He pulls at his collar. "It's Richard. And I drive a yellow Trans Am."

Of course he does. I take another bite of food, chew it slowly, and swallow. "I hope you don't speed through town."

"Uh… uh…" he starts to mutter, and I just stare at him, letting him know exactly what I think of him.

My dad is looking between Dick and me, and he knows something's up.

Dick clears his throat. "Cassie, I was thinking after dinner, you and I could talk."

I tense, and Cassie is already shaking her head. "We don't have anything to talk about."

He's not giving up, though. He's terrible at reading the room. "But we do. I wanted to apologize to you."

Cassie laughs. "What exactly are you apologizing for? Pressuring me to have sex with you, cheating on me, or the fact that you got caught cheating on me? Which of those things are you actually wanting to apologize for?"

Brandi raises her voice. "Cassie, now, honey, everyone makes mistakes."

My mouth drops, and I can't hold it in any longer. "Are you for real right now?"

Cassie is looking at her mom like she doesn't understand what's happening, and I can't say I blame her. I don't understand this at all.

"Mom, if you think I want to sit across the dinner table from him, knowing what he did to me, then you're crazy."

"Crazy!" her mom screams. "I'm not crazy."

Brook is sitting across the table with her eyes clenched tightly together. Dick looks as if he's actually enjoying the show, and my dad stands up. "Cassie, is this true? Did he do that to you?"

Brandi stands up. "Now, Ryan—"

My dad cuts her off. "No, I won't sit down and be silent anymore. She's your daughter, Brandi. I don't understand."

He's shaking his head, trying to wrap his thoughts around it. He straightens to his full height. "You hurt my daughter and then come to my table, my house… get the hell out of here."

I jump up from my seat and make my way around to where Dick is sitting. He stands up, and I use my body to push him out of the room. My dad follows me, and we follow Dick all the way outside to his car.

CHAPTER 21
CASSIE

I'M SITTING HERE SPEECHLESS. When I hear the front door slam, I turn to my mom. "I told you what he did to me. I told you that he was pressuring me to have sex."

She rolls her eyes. "You're twenty-two, Cassie. Grow up."

I rear back as if she slapped me. "Grow up? You're telling me to grow up! Mom, he cheated on me—"

She cuts me off. "Because you wouldn't put out."

Brook stands up from the table. "Mother!"

I shake my head and hold my hand up. "It's fine, Brook. It's not like we don't know how she is." I turn to my mom. "I just wish one time you'd be on our side."

Her face twists in anger. "Your side? What have you always wanted, Cassie? A family. And now what? I gave you one, and you're the one that's screwing it all up."

"Me? I'm going to screw it up?" I ask in outrage.

She puts her hands on her hip. "Yes. I know you're fucking your stepbrother."

I gasp in shock, but she's not finished. "If anything, you're the one that's tearing this family apart."

It sucks that she's throwing this in my face. I knew if she ever found out, she would, and I was right. But I refuse to back down. She's putting the blame on me when she's the one that started all this tonight. "I'm not going to tear up anything."

She laughs bitterly. "You think if you put out to him, he's going to stay? He's not going to stay, Cassie. If I've taught you nothing else, I've taught you that. And I have to ask you… is it worth it?"

Brook has walked around the table and is standing next to me, hugging me. It's always been like this. We've always had to have each other's backs. We've learned through the years that if nothing else, we have each other.

The front door opens, and Ryan and Baker come in. Ryan comes straight to me and hugs me. His voice is soft and soothing, and I start to cry instantly. "I know I'm not your dad, Cassie, but I think of you as my daughter. I will always be here for you, and if someone hurts you, I'll take care of it." He leans back and looks in my face. "Anyone," he says.

I sniff, and he lets me go and hugs Brook, telling her the same thing.

My mom throws a napkin down on the table. "Oh, Ryan, for fuck's sake, they bring this on themselves. I'm done. You all have ruined a perfect dinner."

She stomps out of the room, and we all ignore her tantrum.

Brook says she's leaving, and I hug her bye. As Ryan walks her out, Baker reaches for my hand. I pull back and cross my arms over my chest. Right now, I hate my mom. It doesn't feel good thinking that, but I do. But if there is something she's taught me, it's that men leave. Who knows how much longer Ryan is going to put up with her shit? And then there's Baker. I've already proven I'm way more trouble than I'm worth. He'll be gone next, and I have no doubt my heart will shatter.

There's real fear in Baker's eyes when he says my name. "Cassie? Go pack a bag. You're coming to stay with me."

I hold myself tighter. "I can't."

He takes a step toward me, and I take a step back. He's shocked. "What do you mean you can't?"

"I think we need to pause for a minute."

He clenches his eyes shut and then peels them open. "Pause?"

Fuck, I know it sounds ridiculous. "Yes, pause. It's not worth tearing our family apart when you're going to leave me anyway."

It's like nothing is computing, and he's just repeating things I say. "Leave you?"

I nod. "Yes. When you're tired of me—heck, I'm tired of me already—you'll leave."

He blows out a breath, and I can see the anger on his face. "Tired of you?"

The tears start to well up again, and I don't even try to hold them back. "Yes, we both know it's going to happen."

He runs his hand through the scruff of his chin. "Cassie, are you hearing yourself right now? You just said I'm not worth it. That what we have is not worth it."

I shake my head. "I didn't mean it like that."

He looks so angry, and each word he says his voice is hard and void of emotion. "I was ready to put you first. I know how I feel, but I can't fight your past. Your dad was a shitty dad. Your ex was a shitty boyfriend. I'm not him. I'm not them."

I start to sob, and it wracks my body. I try to stop, but I can't control it.

He's mad, but he still pleads with me. "Please, stop crying, Cass. I can't stand to see you cry, and you're going to get another migraine."

It's then I know I've messed up. I can feel the anger vibrating off him, but he's more concerned about me than letting that stop him from making sure I'm okay. "Cassie, what I want more than anything is to hold you right now, but you don't want to let me. I'm going to leave because then maybe you'll stop crying. Let me know when you're done with this 'pause.'"

With his hands fisted at his sides, he walks away. Before he crosses over the threshold, he stops but doesn't look at me. "Don't forget to take your medicine and put an ice pack on your head."

He's out the door when I cry out his name. "Baker!"

But he doesn't stop. When the door slams shut, I drop to my knees in agony. *What have I done?*

CHAPTER 22
BAKER

I ALMOST CALLED IN TODAY.

I wanted to, but I knew if I stayed home, I would go crazy. So here I am at the station being an asshole to anyone that tries to talk to me.

I've tried to convince myself that it's fine and Cassie will come to her senses, but it's been over twenty-four hours and not a peep. I did talk to my dad just to check on her, and he told me she went to bed last night with a migraine but was better this morning when she left for school.

There's a knock on my door, and I call out, almost angry that I'm being interrupted from my thoughts of Cassie, "What?"

Shit, I know I need to check my attitude, but right now everyone's going to have to put up with 'asshole Baker.'

My sergeant opens the door and levels me with a look. JB has been my mentor since I started the force. He was my only contact to the outside world when I was undercover. He's a brilliant man, and I've learned a lot from him. He definitely doesn't deserve my attitude.

"I'm about to go across town and check something out. Can you walk me out?"

I sigh and put my hands on the top of my desk and push myself up. This isn't the first time he's asked me to walk him out. Sometimes it's to invite me to dinner with him and his wife, and sometimes it's when he wants to talk to me about something private.

I follow him outside, and the whole walk to his car, he doesn't say a word.

When we stop next to the squad car, he crosses his arms over his chest. "All right, spill it."

Confused, I ask him, "You wanted to talk to me."

He nods knowingly. "Yeah, to figure out what's going on with you. You've been preoccupied, and you know you can't do that with this job."

I know he's right, but I still try to defend myself. "This is Whiskey Run, JB."

He raises a hand and points at me, "Yeah, bad things happen everywhere."

Fuck, I know he's right. From my years on the force, I know that bad things can happen at any time, anywhere. I have no excuse to act the way I'm acting now. I can save my bad mood for home. Here, on the job, I need to be alert. For my own safety and the safety of my brothers in blue.

"I know. And you're right. I'll get my shit together."

He tilts his head and looks at me with doubt. JB and I know each other well, and I know he's not going to stop until I talk to him and tell him what's going on with me. "I told you about Cassie."

He nods, encouraging me to go on. I know that Cassie and I weren't going to tell anyone about us, but JB guessed there was something going on the night that Colby ran away. He said he saw sparks flying between us, and I believe him. "Well, she said she wanted us to 'pause' last night." I run my hand through my hair. "Hell, I don't even know what 'pause' means."

He's quiet, waiting for me to continue. "She's afraid it will mess with our family. She thinks I'm just going to dump her in a few weeks and we should just end it now."

"Damn, you're so crazy for her it's almost sickening, Baker. I've never seen you like this."

I shrug because it's the truth. I am crazy for her, and even now when she told me she wanted to 'pause,' I knew I wasn't going to let her end it. I'm hoping she'll think about it and come to her senses.

I can see the thoughts whirling in his head. "So she's scared. That's what it all comes down to. She's having all these feelings, and she's afraid you don't feel the same. That's what it sounds like to me." He pauses and gestures to me. "Did you tell her how you feel about her?"

"She knows." But as soon as I say it, I question if I'm right or not. There's a really big chance that she doesn't have a clue how I feel about her. She may not realize how fuckin' special it is when we come together. I'm her first, and maybe she thinks all this is just normal. Well, I've got news—none of this is normal. Every interaction I've had with her is special and unique. I shake my head. *Damn, she doesn't know.*

JB chuckles. "You don't even have to say it. I can tell by the look on your face that you haven't told her. What the hell, Baker?"

I put my hands on my hips and shake my head. He's right, and I hate to tell him that because I'll never live it down, but he won't leave until I tell him. "You're right. Fuck, I hate to say it but you're right. She doesn't know, and I didn't tell her."

JB crosses his arms over his chest. "Twenty-five years of marriage and I've learned a few things. Hang with me and I'll teach you."

"Yeah, yeah, you're right. I said it. Don't rub it in."

He laughs out loud and slaps me on the shoulder. "You want something bad enough, you gotta work for it, Baker. You know that."

I nod as he starts to walk around to the driver's side. "Where you off to anyway?"

"Remember Mrs. Morrison?"

I nod my head. She's a single mom of three. Her ex-con husband is in jail for possession of a gun and a schedule one narcotic. "Yeah, I remember her."

He leans his arms on the top of his squad car. "Well, Mr. Morrison got out of jail today. I'm not sure how it happened, but I wanted to go make sure she knew since she turned him in. Knowing Tony, I'm sure he hasn't forgiven her. We need to up patrol around her neighborhood for a bit."

I put my hand on my holster. "I can go and check on her."

He shakes his head. "No, I told her I'd come personally if I heard anything."

I step back from the car. "See you, Sarge."

"See you," he says as he gets in.

I grab my phone and am about to call Cassie, but I know that telling her how I feel about her is not something I should do on the phone. No, I need to do it in person. After my shift, I'll go by Dad's house and climb up the tree again. I just hope she lets me in.

CHAPTER 23
CASSIE

FROM THE TIME I walked in the door after school, I've been in my room. I have yet to talk to my mother, and I'm not looking forward to it. I'm done. Looking back, I should have found a way to get myself out of here before this, but I'm determined to do it now. I'll leave and then I'll mend things with Baker. If he'll have me.

I'm on my laptop, looking at the slim picking of apartments available in Whiskey Run when I shut it in frustration. I hate to do it, but I'm going to have to talk to Brook and see if she can find an apartment through Walker. He owns half the town anyway. Maybe he has an apartment coming available.

I hear my stepdad's phone ring, and I jump out of my seat. I go to stand in the hallway and strain to hear him talk. I'm pretty sure I heard him talking to Baker earlier, and so now I'm shamelessly listening anytime I hear his phone ring.

"What?"

"Where?"

"The hospital in Jasper?"

I can only hear my stepdad's side of the conversation, but it's easy to tell that he's in panic mode.

My stomach drops and I run into my room and throw on my shoes before running downstairs. Ryan is grabbing his keys off the entry table, and when he looks at me, he looks as if he's aged around twenty years. "What is it? Is Baker okay?"

His voice is shaky, and he drops the keys on the ground. "He was in an accident."

I pick up the keys. "An accident?"

Ryan leans against the table and is white as a sheet. "He's been shot. I don't know all the details. If they told me, I don't remember. Oh my God, I promised Lorraine I would take care of our son, and he's been shot."

I grab on to Ryan and help him stand up straight again. "Ryan, he's going to be okay. He has to be okay. Come on, I'll drive."

We're almost out the door when Ryan remembers my mom. "Brandi," he bellows. "Baker's been shot and is in the hospital."

She comes out of the kitchen and looks out of patience. "I have cookies in the oven."

Shock registers on my stepdad's face, and I understand how he's feeling. I've had this exact feeling a thousand times when it comes to my mom. But we don't have time to deal with her right now. "Ryan, let's go."

Without another word, Ryan and I walk out the door. I'm running to my car, practically dragging him with me. I know he's in shock, but I can't just leave him to his own devices.

"Jasper Hospital, right?"

He nods, and I peel out of the driveway.

We make it to the hospital in Jasper in record time. I park haphazardly in an emergency lane, and we run in. Already the waiting room is full of men and women in blue. One of the guys comes up to us. "Sergeant, how's my son?" Ryan asks.

The man grabs on to Ryan's upper arms. "He's in surgery right now. He was shot twice. Once in the vest. Once in the shoulder. They've extracted the bullet, and they said he has a concussion from when he hit his head."

I'm holding my breath. I don't want details right now. The only thing that matters to me is if he's going to live or not. "He's going to be okay?"

The man seems to notice me for the first time. "Cassie?"

I nod. "Yeah."

He puts his hand on my shoulder. "He's going to be okay. He'll probably be doing better when he finds out you're here."

All I can do is nod my head. Ryan puts his arm around my shoulder. "Now we wait. Let's have a seat."

We sit down in the closest seats, and I stare at the door that leads to the back. Ryan grabs my hand. "He's going to be okay, honey. He's strong."

I suck back a sob. I'm barely holding on. I felt like I had to be strong to get us here, and now I just feel completely numb. "I broke up with Baker."

I don't know why I admit it. I'm not sure what all Ryan knows about Baker and me, but I'm sure he figured something was going on.

He holds my hand. "I figured something happened when he pulled out of the house yesterday. Needless to say, he wasn't happy."

When I don't say anything, he asks, "Why did you break up with him?"

Still staring at the door that leads to the back, I mumble, "Because he would break up with me anyway. When he finds out what a mess I am, he'll dump me. He's my stepbrother, and Mom said I was ruining the family—"

He cuts me off by leaning in, putting his shoulder against mine. "You love him, don't you? And it scares the hell out of you?"

The tears start to fall, and no matter how much I wipe at them and try to get a hold of myself, I can't stop crying. "I do. I love him."

He reaches over and puts his arm around my shoulder. "Then you'll make it work."

I blink, and more tears roll down my cheeks. I give up trying to stop them and just give in to the fact that I'm going to cry. At least until I see Baker with my own eyes and know he's okay. "But you and Mom… he's my stepbrother and I don't want—"

He cuts me off, and there's nothing but compassion in his voice. "Oh, Cassie, how long have you had to take care of everyone else? You just need to focus on you and what you want. Do what makes you happy."

"What if—?" I start.

He shakes his head. "Honey, I know it's scary. Trusting someone else with your heart is probably one of the hardest things you'll ever do. But I'll tell you this: You'll regret it if you don't try."

I don't want to say it, but I've thought it the whole night. I royally messed up last night, and who knows what Baker's thinking now? "What if he changed his mind? What if he's decided I'm not worth it?"

I barely get the words out and the door to the back opens. Every man and woman in blue rise to their feet, and I stand up with Ryan's help.

"Family of Baker Johnson?"

Ryan looks around the room. "It's us. All of us."

The surgeon nods his head and takes his hat off. He's grim and straight to the point. "The surgery was successful. He'll have to stay for a day or two, and when he goes home he'll need to be monitored. Our worries now are infection and the concussion."

He drones on about the ins and outs of the surgery, and I know I should be paying better attention, but the only thing I need right now is to see him. I have to get to wherever he is.

I interrupt the doctor. "Can we see him now?"

He looks around the room and then back at Ryan and me. "Yes, two of you can go back at a time. He's going to be groggy." He points to the doors. "Down the hall. Room 117."

I start walking, and Ryan stays right beside me. I hear the doctor talking to the other police officers, but once the door closes behind us, the only sounds are the beeps of machines as we pass by rooms. When we get to 117, I stop and shudder a breath. Ryan gently shoves me toward the door. "Go on, sweetie. I'm going to give you a few minutes."

I shake my head. "No, he'll want to see you."

He nods knowingly. "And he will, but trust me. More than anything, he'll want to see you right now."

I push through the door, and the sight of him brings tears to my eyes again. He's hooked up to all kinds of machines, and he's so pale I hold my hand to my mouth to silence my whimper. He's asleep, and I'm not going to wake him up. I open the door a crack and wave for Ryan to come in. "He's asleep."

Ryan sits down in one of the chairs, and I move across the room and lean against the wall. I watch Baker closely, counting between breaths, watching his chest rise and fall. I can't take my eyes off him.

When he stirs in his sleep and moans, I move to his side. I lay my hand on his just because I have to touch him. I need to have my hands on him.

He opens his eyes, and when his brown eyes meet mine, I see the pain in their depths. He looks around in confusion. In a soft whisper, I tell him, "You're going to be okay. You were shot. But you're going to be okay."

He nods and in a strangled voice he asks, "JB?"

Ryan comes up beside me. "He's fine, son. He's in the lobby waiting to see you."

I squeeze his hand. "They said there can only be two back here at a time. I can go so he can come back."

He turns his hand and laces our fingers together. "Don't leave."

I sob and nod my head.

All I can do is stare at Baker as he and his dad talk. There are so many things I need to say, but all I can do is look at him and be thankful that he's still here with me.

CHAPTER 24
BAKER

I CAN SEE how worried my dad is. I know this is hard for him. He hasn't been in a hospital since my mom died, and I'm sure this is bringing back memories for him. He's not looking good. "You okay, Dad?"

He leans down and kisses the top of my head. "I am, son. I'm okay now that I know you're okay."

Cassie sobs, and I squeeze her hand. "I'm okay, Cass. Don't cry, you're going to get another migraine."

And she cries harder. She's apologizing as she ferociously wipes her face with the backs of her hands. "I'm fine. I'm going to get a tissue."

I release her reluctantly, and she walks into the bathroom. I look at my dad. "You're sure you're okay?"

He sniffs too. "Yeah, I'm okay, son."

Cassie comes back in the room with a box of tissues in her hand. It's obvious she tried to stop crying, but the damage is done. Her eyes are red and swollen, and she's squinting, which is a perfect tell that she's getting a migraine. "You okay?"

She nods, leaning against the wall. My dad looks between the two of us. "I want you both to know that no matter what, I'm your dad. I'll always be here for you both… no matter what."

Groggily, I answer him. "I know that, Dad."

He turns to Cassie, who is crying all over again. He says, "That goes for you too, sweetie."

She walks over to my dad, and I watch as they hug. She's so emotional, and it's not going to help her with her headache. "Has she been like this the whole time?"

My dad blushes. "Well, I sort of panicked, and she had to drive me here. But yeah, once we got here and she found out you were okay, she's been like this."

I hold my hand out to her. "Come here."

She walks to me, holding her hand out. "Get up here."

She shakes her head. "I'll hurt your—"

I cut her off. "Woman, quit arguing with everything I say. Please, get up here."

She walks around to the other side, where I'm not injured, and she gently climbs into the bed. I pull her into my side, and she rests her head on my shoulder and her hand on my abdomen. I kiss the top of her forehead. "Close your eyes and try to rest."

Dad watches us with happiness on his face. He knows how I feel about her. He may not know exactly, but I'm sure he has an idea.

We're all quiet when there's a commotion out in the hall. I tense until I see it's Brook forcing her way through the door. "What the hell happened? Why did no one call me?"

Cassie raises her head and winces. "I'm sorry. I should have called you, sis."

She hugs Ryan and looks around the room. "Where's Mom?"

I shrug because I don't know, and Ryan looks down at the floor. Cassie's the one that answers. "She didn't come. She was in the middle of something." She raises her head to look at me. "Don't take it personal.

She's never been the type to be there for people. It's not you."

I run my hand through her hair, pushing it off her face. "You don't have to apologize for her. My three favorite people are here. I'm good."

Brook threads her arm through Ryan's. "I get you in the divorce, Dad."

"Brooklyn," Cassie admonishes.

She shrugs. "What? We're all thinking it."

Luckily, Dad doesn't take offense and actually laughs. He and Brook talk, and I whisper to Cassie. "You okay? Want me to get you some meds for your head?"

She searches my eyes with shock registered on her face. "How is it you're hurt, and you're worried about me? I should be asking you if you're okay."

I want to tell her. I want to tell her that I love her and that I'll always worry about her, but with Brook and Ryan watching us, I don't. I do squeeze her closer to me. "No matter what—if you're in my arms, I'm good."

If anything, she buries herself deeper into my side. "That's good because I'm not leaving."

I listen to Brook and my dad talk about her new job. She keeps turning, watching her sister in my arms, but she seems happy about it.

"When can I get out of here?"

My dad laughs. "Well, the doctor said a day or two. I can't wait to see them try to keep you here."

I shake my head. "I'm not lying in this bed for two days. There's no way."

Dad looks worried. "One day. Let them check you tomorrow and then you can ask to be released."

I'm about to tell him no when he pleads with me. "Son, please. Will you do this for me?"

I sigh because my dad knows I have trouble telling him no. "Fine. One day. Tomorrow, I'm out of here. You can go on home and get some rest. Maybe bring me some clothes back tomorrow. Do you still have my extra set of house keys?"

Dad nods. "I do. But I'm not sure how I'm getting home."

"I can get you," Brook says. "Walker insisted on driving me here, so I can just have him drop you off at home."

Dad's eyes light up. "Walker? Is he driving his big 'Boss' truck?"

Brook scrunches up her nose. "The white one?"

Dad and I both roll our eyes, and Dad tells her, "Yeah, the white one."

"Then yeah, that's what he's driving."

My dad seems almost giddy to get to be riding in Walker's big rig. He comes over to stand next to the bed. "You're sure you're okay?"

I gesture to Cassie in my arms. "I'm good, Dad. I promise."

He leans down and kisses the top of my head and then does the same to Cassie. "You two take care of each other."

"We will," I assure him.

Cassie murmurs the same.

Brook comes over next and side-hugs both of us. "See you, sis. See you, bro."

I hear the teasing tone in her voice and Cassie does too because she sticks her tongue out at her.

Before they leave, I tell Dad, "Can you tell JB and everyone I'm okay, that I just need to rest?"

"I will, son. I'll see you in the morning. Love you both."

"Love you," I call after him.

"Love you," Cassie says softly and with her voice full of emotion.

We lie here for a few minutes before I ask her, "Do you want to talk?"

Her reply is instant. "No. Can you just hold me, Baker?"

"Yes." I whisper against her head before I kiss it. I'm not sure what's coming tomorrow, but I'm going to enjoy having her in my arms tonight.

CHAPTER 25
CASSIE

"You go back to work tomorrow."

He doesn't have to remind me, though. For the last week, I've dreaded this day, knowing I'd have to go back to work and leave him. To cover up my worry and sadness, I joke with him. "Are you sick of me already?"

I've been with him for seven days straight, twenty-four hours a day. I probably could have left him long enough to go to the store or run errands, but I didn't want to. Luckily, Ryan has been more than helpful. He packed up some of my clothes and bathroom items and brought them over. He's gone to the store and stocked the fridge. And he's brought over takeout. He's come by every day, and I get more of a glance each time what I was missing having a dad growing up.

Baker gives me a penetrating look and grabs my hand. 'You know I'm not sick of you."

I grin, but it doesn't quite meet my eyes. Even though we've been together for a week, we haven't really talked about anything too personal, and it's driving me crazy. There are so many things I want to get off my chest. "And you have probably another month before you get released for light duty."

He shrugs because he doesn't want to argue. He's already tried to tell me that he's going back to work next week. I ignore his shrug. "A month. I have talked to Ryan and Brook. They're both coming at different times to check on you and make sure everything is okay. I'll be here after school, but if you need anything, just call me and I'll come."

He's sitting on the couch, watching me move around. I'm just trying to stay busy because I'm feeling antsy. "Stop," he says and holds his hand out. "Come here and talk to me."

But I don't take it. I stack some magazines on the coffee table and act as if I have to clean up when almost every corner of his house is immaculate.

His hand drops. "Brook said that Walker has an apartment that opened up."

I nod and avoid looking at him. "Yeah, I'm going to go look at it this week. It's time for me to move out. After talking to your dad this week, I don't think he and Mom are doing well. But I don't blame him. I think the fact she didn't come to the hospital was the breaking point for him." I lift my eyes to Baker, embarrassed about how my mom is behaving. "I tried talking to her the other day and told her she was messing up. You can imagine how she took it. Anyway, I think your dad is better off. He deserves a woman that loves him more than anything."

"Cassie," he says.

I finally turn around and look at him. "Yeah? You need something?"

He nods. "Yeah, I need you to come over here and sit down and talk to me."

I walk over and sit on the couch. "Have you liked staying here this week with me?"

I draw patterns into the seat cushion between us. "You know I have."

He sighs in frustration. "I don't know because any time I try to talk to you, you change the subject."

Ashamed, I lower my head. I've tried to soak this whole week in. Every bit of it I've tried to commit to memory because I'm afraid at any point he's going to tell me to leave. "Do you remember what happened between me and you before everything?"

"There's nothing wrong with my memory. You mean the 'pause'?"

I shudder, remembering the fight we had. The way he looked when he thought I was telling him he wasn't worth it. And the whole time, I was scared. I need to come clean because I'll regret it if I don't. "I was scared, Baker. I thought you would leave me anyway. I didn't want to hurt you or come between you and your dad."

His gaze bores into me. "And so what? You're taking care of me because I'm your stepbrother? Is that it?"

"No. Of course not."

"Then why?" he challenges.

Looking at him, I know I need to be brave. I move closer to him, and he reaches for my hand. His touch gives me the confidence to say what I need to say. "I'm going to tell you something, and I want you to know that you don't have to say anything. I just need to let you know."

He tenses and looks at me apprehensively, but I continue. "I love you, Baker. I know I said that we shouldn't do this and nothing could come of us, but I fell for you. Every day of these last few weeks you've shown me how it feels to be loved, cherished, and taken care of. I don't want to lose what we have and—"

His voice is husky as he cuts me off. "You love me?"

I bring my hand up and cup his jaw. "How could I not, Baker? You're the one that showed me what love is."

He brings his forehead to mine, and I can hear the emotion in his voice. "Fuck, I love you. I love you so much."

I gasp, and he pulls back to look at me with his soulful brown eyes. "How did you not know, Cass? From the moment I met you, I knew."

He claims my lips and crushes me to him. I kiss him, putting every ounce of love I feel for him into it.

He groans, and I jerk back. "Your shoulder."

His gaze is intense as he stares at me. "Not my shoulder. Woman, you've lain next to me in bed for a week, snuggled up to me, and I need you."

I shake my head, looking at his injury with concern. "I don't want to hurt you."

He's about to argue with me when I pull from his hold and stand up. "That means you're just going to have to sit there and let me take care of you."

I go to my knees on the floor in front of him and reach for the button of his pants. His hand goes to mine to stop me. "I want to be inside you."

I smirk. "I can arrange that."

"And…" he starts.

I slowly unbutton his jeans and lower the zipper. I motion for him to raise up so I can pull his pants down, but he's not budging. "And you're moving in here with me."

My eyes fly to his. "You want me to move in here… with you?"

He laughs. "Yeah. I want you with me, Cass. I want to spend every day with you, showing you what real love feels like."

My mind starts to whirl, and my past insecurities come to a head. "What if—"

He leans forward. "What if we live happily ever after?"

A soft gasp escapes me. "I want that so bad. I want you to be mine forever."

He cups my cheeks. "I'm yours, Cass, and I always will be."

"Yes," I say with a startled gasp. For the first time in a long time, I'm going after what I want. "Yes, I'll move in with you."

I raise up so I can reach his lips, and we kiss again. When I pull back, the bulge of his manhood is standing erect between us. I cup him through his jeans, and he groans. "We can talk later about the ring and all the babies we're going to have."

"Ring! Babies!" I exclaim.

He laughs and finally raises up so I can pull his pants down. He wraps his hand around his length and pumps himself. It's hard to concentrate with him doing that right in my face. "I want it all with you, Cass. I want everything."

With love shining in my eyes, I have to agree. "Me too."

I wrap my hand around his girth and look into his eyes. "This just feels right, Baker. Everything with you feels right."

He threads his fingers through my hair, pushing it off my face. "Damn right it does, baby."

EPILOGUE
CASSIE

"I still can't believe you planned all this without me knowing."

"Do you like it?"

I look around at all the other booths and then back at mine. "Baker, this is the best booth here."

He puffs out his chest with pride. I'm not joking, though. He really did create the best booth at the carnival. It's all pink and shiny. I have no idea how he came up with the idea, but it's perfect.

He puts an arm around my shoulder. "I pulled some strings and got my booth right next to you too. I can't have all these single dads hanging out over here. Not on my watch."

I slap him on the chest with a laugh. "What a joke. You have made it clear to everyone in Whiskey Run that I'm taken."

He laughs with a shrug. "Well, you can never be too careful. I can't have someone thinking they may have a chance."

I turn in his arms and wrap my arms around his waist. The gymnasium is full of people, but I don't care. Like Baker, I have made sure to tell everyone that he's mine.

I lean back and look at his tanned face. "Our spring break was weeks ago. I can't believe how tan you still are."

We spent a week at the beach, and it was perfect. It was another surprise that Baker sprang on me. He leans down and kisses my forehead. "And your burn is finally fading."

The memories come in fast and hard. "Yeah, well, it's not your fault. You were applying sunscreen to my body every chance you got."

"I had my motives."

I can't help but laugh.

"So do you like the booth?"

"Like it? I love it."

He pulls me in between our two booths so we're out of sight. Everyone is still setting up and paying us no mind.

He wraps his arms around me and kisses me fiercely. "I love you," he whispers when he pulls back.

"I love you too." These last few months have been amazing. I did end up moving in with him, and I have not regretted it once. Our parents' marriage is over, but they've both moved on and are fine. My mom moved into Jasper, and we really don't see her a lot. Ryan still lives in the same house a few streets over. He and my sister Brook come to dinner at our house every Sunday.

I settle in his arms, content in just staying here right where I'm at. That's probably one of my favorite things about Baker is that he knows how to hold me. "I have one more surprise."

I smile as the sounds of kids coming into the gymnasium start to echo off the walls. "You're spoiling me, Baker Johnson."

He kisses me again. "I hope so. So do you want to see your booth in action?"

"I do."

He leads me to the front of the booth, and the kids from my classroom are all standing in a semi-circle outside of the booth. They're lit up and excited, and I can't blame them. This carnival is going to be amazing. "Hey guys! Are you ready to have some fun?"

Colby calls out, "Yes!"

I raise my hand to give him a high-five, and he slaps it excitedly.

"You guys want a turn? Officer Johnson is just about to show me how our booth works!"

Kaitlyn, always the rule follower, throws her hand up. "Miss Waters, we want to watch you."

I point at myself. "Me? All right, kids, I'm going to show you how it's done."

I turn to walk inside my booth and am still amazed at everything that's in it. There are things everywhere. Different knick-knacks, puzzles, pictures, song lyrics. Everything is red and pink, and there's a big sparkly chandelier hanging in the middle. "Okay, I'm ready." I turn to the kids standing outside of the booth and give them all a thumbs-up.

Baker starts to go over the rules. "Okay, welcome to Treasure Quest. You have five minutes to solve five puzzles. I'll give you clues, and you have to walk around the room and find the answer or solve a puzzle. You answer correctly, you win the treasure."

I clap my hands together excitedly. "I'm so ready for this."

"Okay, hint number one. This place has our favorite dessert."

I jump up and down excited. "Cinnamon Blaze cake."

He laughs. "Yeah, but you have to find the place we get it."

I start to pace around the room, and when I spot the baseball hat with the Red's Diner logo on it, I raise it up to show him.

"Good job. Okay, hint number two. This is the date when we first met."

My eyes widen. Okay, I start to calculate it, thinking in my head and when I have the answer, I announce it to him. "September tenth."

He laughs again and points to the booth. "You have to find it. You better hurry."

I search the room, and my eyes land on the clock that is set on 9:10. "The clock, the clock. It's set for 9:10."

The kids all cheer in excitement, and I ram my hands in the air in victory.

Baker reads the next card. "You got it. Hint number three, this is where we went on vacation together for the first time."

I search the booth, walking back and forth taking everything in. Finally, I stop in front of a framed picture. It's one I took on our last night on vacation. It's a perfect sunset with the waves crashing in.

I hold it up, and he nods in approval. "Good job."

"Okay hint number four, we're almost done. Find the thing that you're always losing and so I carry one with me so you'll have it."

I bite my lip and smile. "A hair tie." I look around and find a scrunchie lying on the very bottom shelf with some books. I grab it and hold it up. "Found it."

"Okay, last one. What's my favorite thing about you?"

I can feel my face heat and I give him a look. Surely he's not talking about that here in front of all these people. He laughs easily. "The other thing." He looks at his watch. "You better hurry. You have one minute."

I shake my hands in excitement and start searching the booth. On one corner is a mirror and in front of that mirror is a red heart. That's it. That has to be it. He's always saying he loves my heart.

I pick up the box and gasp when I turn to him. Baker is on one knee and grabs my hands holding the box. "Cassie Waters, I love you, and I want to spend the rest of our lives together. Will you please do me the honor of being my wife? Will you marry me?"

He opens the heart box, and inside is the most beautiful diamond ring I've ever seen. Tears are rolling down my cheeks as I tell him "yes" over and over. All the kids start to cheer as Baker puts the ring on my finger. He stands up and encircles me in his arms. His kiss is firm and sweet. He whispers to me as he pulls away, "Tonight when it's just the two of us, we'll celebrate."

"I can't wait."

I look at my ring, and Kaitlyn, unable to control herself, screams, "Show us, Miss Waters!"

I walk out of the booth, and it's then I realize that Brook, Chloe, and Ryan are here, and they saw the whole thing. I walk through the crowd of kids, showing them my ring as they all ooh and ahh over it. My sister hugs me tightly, whispering into my ear, "You deserve this, sis."

Ryan congratulates his son, and Baker pulls him in for a big bear hug. After all the congratulations, the carnival gets into full swing. Baker was prepared and has all kinds of questions for my booth so the kids will be entertained all evening.

When he's stripped down to his swimming trunks for the dunking booth, I have to take a second to catch my breath. "Really? Really? You have a booth where you're going to be half naked all night?"

He laughs. "Yeah, you going to be able to control yourself?"

I shake my head. "You better hope neither Charlotte or any of the other teachers see you like that."

He looks almost guilty. "Cassie, you do know that I raise most of the money because the female teachers buy all my tickets to dunk me."

I gasp. "I did not know that. Are you kidding me right now?"

He looks sheepish. "It's not a big—"

I lean in and kiss him before whispering, "Just remember who you're going home with tonight."

He laughs. "How could I forget? I have the most beautiful fiancée in Whiskey Run, and she's all mine."

I kiss him again. "And you're all mine."

———

Thanks for reading!
If you'd like a bonus epilogue of Baker
and Cassie's story five years later,
download it here: https://authorhopeford.com/
subscribe-to-it-just-feels-right/

If you'd like to read Walker and Brook's story,
read it here: https://mybook.to/RansomHopeFord

Want to read Elias and Chloe's story, read it here:
https://mybook.to/TemptingPromise

Want to know if Haven hires the Cuddler, read her
story here: https://mybook.to/HireACuddler

ALSO BY HOPE FORD

Want more of Whiskey Run?

Whiskey Run

Faithful - He's the hot, say-it-like-it-is cowboy, and he won't stop until he gets the woman he wants.

Captivated - She's a beautiful woman on the run... and I'm going to be the one to keep her.

Obsessed - She's loved him since high school and now he's back.

Seduced - He's a football player that falls in love with the small town girl.

Devoted - She's a plus size model and he's a small town mechanic.

Whiskey Run: Savage Ink

Virile - He won't let her go until he puts his mark on her.

Torrid - He'll do anything to give her what she wants.

Rigid - If you love reading about emotionally wounded men and the women that help them overcome their past, then you'll love Dawson and Emily's story.

Whiskey Run: Cowboys Love Curves

Obsessed Cowboy - She's the preacher's daughter and she's off limits.

Whiskey Run: Heroes

Ransom - He's on a mission he can't lose.

Redeem - He's in love with his sister's best friend.

Submit - She's his fake wife but he wants to make it real.

Forbid - They have a secret romance but he's about to stake his claim.

Whiskey Run: Sugar

One Night Love - Her one night stand wants more.

Rebound Love - She's falling for the rebound guy.

Second Chance Love - He is not a man to ignore... especially when he asks for a second chance.

Bad Boy Love - He's a bad boy that wants her good.

Whiskey Run: Guardians MC

Protective Biker - She needs his protection and he'll give it to her. But he's going to need her heart in exchange.

Broken Biker - There's only one woman for him...

Relentless Biker - He won't stop until he has her back.

Whiskey Men

Reluctant Husband - If you love reading about curvy women getting the hot guy, opposites attract, jealousy trope, marriage of convenience, and small-town romance, then you'll love Lucas and Isabella's story.

Something Real - If you love reading billionaire, single father, age gap, boss/employee, and small-town romance, then you'll love Ford and Lilian's story.

Coming Home - If you love reading billionaire, ex-military, age gap, forced proximity, and small-town romance, then you'll love Hudson and Elle's story.

Forever Mine - If you love reading billionaire, age gap, second chance, and small-town romance, then you'll love Beau and Natalie's story.

Always Yours - If you love reading billionaire, friends to lovers, pregnancy, and small town romance, then you'll love Austin and Ally's story.

JOIN ME!

JOIN MY NEWSLETTER

www.AuthorHopeFord.com/Subscribe

BE A HOTTIE!

JOIN HOPE'S HOTTIES ON FACEBOOK

www.FB.com/groups/hopeford

A place to talk about Hope Ford's books! Find out about new releases, giveaways, get exclusive content, see covers before anyone else and more!

ABOUT THE AUTHOR

USA Today Bestselling Author Hope Ford writes short, steamy, sweet romances. She loves tattooed, alpha men, instant love stories, and ALWAYS happily ever afters.

To find me on Pinterest, Instagram, Facebook, Goodreads, and more:

www.AuthorHopeFord.com/follow-me

Want FREE BOOKS?
Go to www.authorhopeford.com/freebies